To Tell the Truth

Sharon!
Best wishes + keep
reading!
Faye M. Tollison

To Tell the Truth

Faye M. Tollison

ISBN-13 – 978-1461082330

Table of Contents

Chapter 1

Monday, April 8, 2002

Oh God, I don't want to go in there. Please, please don't make me.

The wooden bench in the dimly lit hallway on which Anna Kayce sat was terribly uncomfortable. She felt lonely and scared. A tight squeezing knot in the pit of her stomach left her weak and nauseated. She looked up as heavy oak doors opened, revealing a large, high-ceilinged room. The light from the courtroom spread over the floor of the hallway and worked its way up her silky legs, but then a dark form filled the doorway, obliterating the light. She struggled to focus her eyes.

"Ms. Kayce, they're ready for you," the bailiff said in a stiff voice.

With jelly-like knees she rose from her seat, walked to the doorway, and stopped as the bailiff moved aside to allow her to enter. Efforts had been made to update the old courthouse, built in the 1950's. However, the original ceiling fans and lights hung from the ceiling. As she stood in the doorway, a slight breeze from the fans twirling above ruffled her long, dark hair. Eyes turn to look at her, scrutinizing her, making her feel ill at ease. With difficulty, she turned her attention toward one person in particular.

Prosecutor Thomas Dean Hawthorne maintained his position at the front of the courtroom, his back to her. He stood tall and straight with broad shoulders that drew attention away from his thinning hair. He only did not turn around at her entrance.

A low murmur drifted through the courtroom as Anna stepped inside the door. She hesitated as her gaze swept around the courtroom, coming to rest on the man in a black robe on the far side of the room.

* * *

Judge Edward Cox resided over many court cases in the 27 years he served as a judge, but this was the most famous and exciting one yet. It did not thrill him because he did not like having media in the courtroom much less all these people. They were thrill seekers, most of them anyway. He hoped they would not be rowdy, but it was not looking hopeful. A stern scowl darkened his face.

"Silence! There'll be quiet in this courtroom!" He glared around the room until it became quiet and then nodded his approval. They obviously knew he meant business.

* * *

Inquisitive eyes continued to stare at her, some curious, some with disdain. Most of the people in the room dressed casually; some were dressed in their Sunday best. A mixture of tobacco-scented clothes and sweet perfume permeated the air. Anna turned her gaze to the right side of the room where the jury sat, an even six men and six women. One juror, a young man, smiled at her, then quickly turned his head away, his smile faded as if he had done something he shouldn't. An older woman sat next to him. Her emotionless expression and cold eyes gave Anna an unsettled feeling so Anna quickly moved her gaze on to the next juror. The young woman sitting behind the older lady kept her eyes on the judge, but her glance, as if she were unable to control it, slid to Anna. Unsmiling, she gave a slight nod and turned her attention back to the judge.

They don't understand. They'll never understand...

"She's beautiful," someone whispered.

How insecure I felt then... how insecure I am now.

"Yeah, the senator wouldn't have anything but beautiful," another commented. "Just a high-priced whore's all she is, beautiful or not."

The fear. Oh, God, the fear!

A burning red crawled up her neck and into her face. She had never felt as alone as she did at this moment. Anna took a deep breath, buttoned the jacket of her red suit and grasped a black glove in her other already gloved hand. It's a sign of breeding, the senator once told her. He always insisted she appear well-bred.

"Walk like a lady with your head held high. Someday it will benefit you." His words lingered in her mind. Despite his harsh words at times, he did teach her well.

I hope he's right. Though she felt inadequate to handle what she was about to face, she was able to lift her chin and square her shoulders, eyes held straight ahead of her. *I still do my best to please him—always to please him.*

Eyes and whispers followed her long walk to the witness stand. The gold embossed King James Version seemed to jump at her as she placed her right hand on the Bible held by the bailiff. She swore to tell the truth, the whole truth, and nothing but the truth.

"Please tell the court your name, address, and occupation." The prosecutor stared at the papers in his hand before he laid them on the table in front of him and turned his gaze to her.

Anna stared back at him, eyes unwavering, and in a clear, concise voice answered, "My name is Anna Marie Kayce, spelled K-a-y-c-e. I live at 348 Taylors Drive, apartment number 208, and I own Uptown Styles, Unlimited."

He cleared his throat. His voice firm, flat, he clarified, "A dress shop?"

"Boutique, yes."

"How did you acquire this... boutique?"

"With long hours and hard work."

The prosecutor turned for a moment toward the jury, his brows drawn together, his expression indicated deep thought. Then he faced the witness once again.

"Ms. Kayce, have you ever been married**?"** he asked.

"No."

"Were you acquainted with Senator Kenneth Levall?"

"I knew him, yes."

"How long had you known him?"

"I, uh, I'm not sure."

"Not sure? Surely you have an idea." His tone of voice was mocking. "Just an approximate time that you knew him?"

"I... I don't know... a few years, I guess."

"A few years you guess. Ms. Kayce, I think you know very well how long you were acquainted with the senator, but let's go on. Where did you first meet the senator?"

Anna dropped her gaze and stared at her hands, acutely aware of the quiet that lay heavy across the room. The silence lengthened as the prosecutor waited for her to answer.

"Ms. Kayce, please tell us where you first met the senator." He insisted, obviously losing patience with her.

Anna kept her head lowered, fighting back the tears.

"Your Honor," the prosecutor turned to the judge in exasperation, "this is obviously a hostile witness. I may have to ask leading questions to get the true story from her."

Anna looked up just as Judge Cox looked at the prosecutor with cold steel gray eyes, his face expressionless. His reputation for being hard, compassionless and demanding harsh restrictions on the media in the courtroom was well known by everyone.

"The witness is duly noted for the record to be a hostile witness, Mr. Prosecutor. Proceed with questioning." The judge leaned forward as he spoke, his eyes narrowed as he looked down at the witness. A pained expression passed across Anna's face as she fought to maintain her composure.

The prosecutor turned back to Anna. "Ms. Kayce, once again I'm asking you to tell us where you first met the senator."

"I-I-I think it was at a party." Her voice quivered, and she hated herself for this loss of control.

"Was this party at the senator's home here in Daylan or his home in Washington, D.C.?"

"No, it was at someone else's home here in Daylan."

"Did you contact the senator after the party and encourage the continuation of this new found friendship?"

Anna jerked her head up, eyes wide and blazing. "No! He's the one who called me first."

"And when he called, just what did he say?"

"He said a mutual friend of ours had told him of my financial situation, and he wanted to propose a business arrangement that would be beneficial to both of us. His words, not mine."

"You told him about your financial problems, is that correct?"

"Yes," she said in a low voice.

"Did you do this in hopes of getting some financial help from him or just to make conversation?"

"No, I didn't expect financial help. We were just talking, and it came up."

"I see." A faint hint of sarcasm tainted his voice. "You told him about losing your business, didn't you?"

She looked at him with red, moist eyes. "I lost more than just my business."

"Oh?"

"I lost everything I had. My business, my apartment, my car. I had no money in my checking account. Nada, zilch. There wasn't even enough to get anything to eat. I was totally destitute."

"Go on."

"My parents were dead, my sister was in her final year at college. She had no money to help, not even an apartment to share. My Dad died of cancer, but he ran up a lot of medical bills before he died. Insurance didn't pay them all, so I had hospital bills coming out of my ears. Mom lived for a year after Dad's death. She just seemed to fade away. She had no idea how to pay the bills. Dad always did that, so I had to take care of all the financial things for her." She squeezed her eyes closed, causing a tear to tumble down her cheek. "I know you can't understand how it was for me, but I was destitute and desperate. The senator's proposal was my lifesaver. I felt I had no choice but to accept it." She raised a trembling hand to wipe away the tear.

"Exactly what was this *beneficial* business arrangement?" The prosecutor waited for her to answer while a tense silence lay heavy over the room.

Her eyes glared with anger as she looked first at the prosecutor, swung her gaze to the jury, then toward the judge.

"Okay," the prosecutor said, "let me rephrase that. Did you have an affair with the senator as a result of this... *arrangement?"*

"An affair? Not exactly." Her insides tightened into knots, but her hands lay still in her lap. She managed with difficulty to keep her voice steady.

"What do you mean not exactly? Either you did, or you didn't."

"You don't—can't understand."

"I see. Then once again let me rephrase. Did you have an intimate relationship with the senator?" He walked closer to her and positioned himself with his back to the courtroom but where she would be in full view of the jury.

Be careful, don't trust him. "Uh..." She heard the slight quiver in her voice. "Yes." The slight upward curve of his mouth was the only indication that he noticed her nervousness.

She followed his slow deliberate strides to the jury box where he faced the jurors, his forefinger tapping his chin. The silent, suffocating tension built around her. She waited.

"Did you love him?" He said in a low voice, his back still toward her.

"What?" Her brows drew together in puzzled disbelief.

He turned slowly and looked at her with narrowed eyes. "I asked you if you loved the senator. Actually, Ms. Kayce—"

"Anna," she said, "please, call me Anna." She was tired of his formality, but more than anything she wanted this nightmare to end.

"Actually, it was a business arrangement. Isn't that correct?"

"You don't understand," she said, anger edging her voice.

"Your Honor." Defense Attorney Larry Davis rose from his chair, stretching his body to its full height of six feet and three inches. "I realize this is the prosecutor's own witness, but please, let the witness answer one question before another is asked."

"Yes, Counselor, I agree." The judge said. "Objection sustained."

"Did you love him?" The prosecutor asked again.

"I-I did at one time—at the beginning."

"But it was a business arrangement, was it not?"

"If you insist on calling it that, yes."

"Just a yes or no, please."

"Yes."

"Was the senator married at the time you first met him?" he asked.

"He told me he was divorced, but I found out later it was not final."

"So technically he was still married at the time you began this business arrangement."

Since this was not a question, Anna chose not to answer.

"Did this not matter to you?" His voice was gentle, but his eyes coldly held hers.

"Yes, technically he was still married, but the marriage was finished. It was just a matter of getting the paperwork done. So, no, it really didn't bother me since I had no intention of marrying him."

The prosecutor lowered his eyes, and Anna waited patiently. The silence lengthened. After a few moments, he looked up and said, "Do you know the defendant, Detective John Mentz?"

"John? Yes, I know him."

"You had an affair with him, did you not?"

Anna blinked and averted her gaze. "We had a relationship."

"A relationship? One that was not a business arrangement?" The prosecutor glanced toward the jury, a small smile conveying confidence his point was made.

"Yes." Her voice was low but well heard.

"You were present when the senator was murdered, were you not?"

Her mouth opened but closed without saying anything. She knew the direction his questioning was going and dreaded it.

"Weren't you, Ms. Kayce?" The prosecutor became more insistent.

"Yes, I was."

"And you saw Detective Mentz kill the senator. Is that correct?"

"No! I did not." Her answer was quick, her voice louder, more confident.

"Are you sure about that? He confessed to killing the senator, and you admit to being present at the time. Be very sure, Ms. Kayce, before you answer."

She stared at the prosecutor, her look deliberate, unmoving. Her hands trembled in her lap, but she held her head high, chin defiantly uplifted. *I must face my demons... and my enemies. I must!*

After a few moments, the judge leaned forward and looked down at Anna. "Answer the question, please," he instructed.

Anna acknowledged the judge's command but kept her gaze locked on the prosecutor. He was the first to shift his eyes from her defiant stare. Turning his back to her, he walked to the prosecutor's table.

"No." Her voice cut through the tense silence. "I did not see John kill Ken."

The prosecutor stopped mid-stride and paused before slowly turning around to face her.

"Who killed him, Ms. Kayce?"

Anna struggled to sit up straighter and turned her gaze toward the jurors, her eyes wide and moist. She could feel the tense expectation in the air, and she knew they wanted – no expected to hear who the murderer was. In a quivery voice, she said, "I honestly don't know."

"Who held the gun?"

She pressed her lips together before her low voice said, "I did."

A low murmur and the shuffling of feet broke the tense silence of the courtroom.

"We *will* have order in this court!" The judge half rose from his chair, pounding his gavel repeatedly.

The prosecutor's long, quick strides brought him close to her, and, hands on the banister, he leaned forward. She could feel his breath on her, could smell the sweet cologne he wore. A nauseated, sinking feeling came over her, and she struggled to control it.

Please, God, let this end soon.

"Detective Mentz said he was the one holding the gun when it went off. He supposedly took it from you. So, Anna, you were there. You claim to be holding the gun at the time it discharged. Just who did kill him, Anna? I think you know, so tell us. Who?" His words cracked through the whispered mutterings, and the room filled with taut silence.

Anna shook her head; her hand clenched the glove she held. The red lipstick glared against the paleness of her skin, and her body shrunk into the chair.

He leaned closer, his face only inches from hers.

"Anna, tell us what happened that night. Tell us the truth."

Chapter 2

Wednesday, November 14, 2000

The telephone rang several times. Just as Anna was about to hang up, there was the click of the receiver being lifted.

"Hi," she said.

"Well, hello." Senator Kenneth Levall's voice changed from cold terseness to a more welcoming, warm tone when he heard her voice.

"Are you busy?"

"Yes, but I have a moment for you."

"I was just thinking about you."

"Mmmm, I like that."

She gave a soft inviting laugh. "I bet I know what you'd like even better."

"I have a feeling you'd be right."

"Will I see you tonight?"

"I have to work late tonight, but I don't think there'll be a problem coming by to see you."

"Good."

"I'll be there around nine. A martini waiting for me when I get there would be nice."

"You'll have it."

"Okay, see you then."

Anna hung up the phone, picked up her purse and jacket, and locked the store. A quick glance at her watch showed the time to be five minutes after seven. Traffic began to get congested, and a light rain started to fall during her drive home. She put in her favorite CD and melted into the traffic. The rain became heavier and harder. It was beginning to get dark, and Anna strained to see the road ahead of her. About halfway home she saw the blue lights of several police cars. Traffic slowed to a crawl. As she drew nearer, Anna saw two cars which had obviously collided. The red lights of an ambulance were flashing, their lights reflecting off the cars close by. She pulled her attention away from the sight and concentrated on the traffic, aware of a headache that was beginning to plague her. The usual twenty-five minute drive home took an hour and ten minutes. Exhausted and relieved to arrive home, she pulled into the garage at her apartment building.

The key slid into the lock and turned easily. She pushed open the door to the apartment and walked across the living room. Just as she reached toward a lamp, strong arms grabbed her, twirled her around, and clasped her against a familiar body. The smell of a man's cologne drifted in the air around her, invoking pleasant memories. She laughed.

"Ken, what are you doing here?"

"My meeting was canceled, so I came on over. Why are you so late?"

"Traffic was terrible, and there was a wreck that held up traffic."

"Poor baby." He kissed her gently on the lips, then on her neck. "But now you are here with me."

She sighed.

"You need to relax. Let me draw you a nice warm bath. While you're soaking, I'll fix a quick dinner. How's that sound?" He pushed a wayward curl away from her eyes, his lips brushed her forehead.

"Irresistible."

"Good."

In the soothing, warm water, Anna felt the tension ease. She slid further into the claw-footed tub until the water covered her tired body all the way to her chin. She wiggled her toes, causing the water to ripple around them, then laid her head back and watched the shadows, created by the light from the candles sitting on the countertop on the other side of the room, dance across the turquoise and white tile. She closed her eyes and enjoyed the contentment. After a while the bathroom door opened, bringing her back from her reverie.

"Dinner's ready." Ken smiled at her, a large fluffy bath towel in his hands.

"Mmm, I'm hungry. What are we having?"

"Well, it's a simple meal, I'm afraid. Pork chops, rice, and a salad."

"Sounds wonderful to me."

"Get dressed. I have a glass of wine waiting for you." He wrapped the towel around her as she got out of the tub, pulled her against him, and gave her a lingering kiss.

"Oh, that's more delicious than any glass of wine."

He laughed as he closed the door behind him.

She toweled her body dry and slipped on a soft pink nightgown. The feel of the silky material against her bare skin felt good. She ran a brush through her hair and joined Ken at the table.

"This is nice," she said.

"I can do okay when I want to."

"Yes, you can. I'm impressed. Dinner looks delicious."

"Thank you." He lifted his glass of wine. "To good relationships and prosperous business."

"Yes, of course... prosperous business." Anna lifted her glass to his.

The conversation was light and bantering. They ate but paid little attention to the food they put in their mouths. Anna often let her eyes take in the handsome man across the table from her. *He's pretending he doesn't notice me admiring him, but I can tell by his coy smile.*

When they had finished eating, Ken rose from his chair and turned on the stereo. The room filled with slow, languid music. He turned to her with a glint in his eyes.

"May I have this dance, Princess?" He held a hand toward her.

"Yes, you may." She placed a hand in his, and he pulled her into his arms. She closed her eyes and allowed her body to sway to his lead, enjoying the feel of his lips as they explored her neck, shoulders, and face.

The music came to a soft melting end, but Anna stayed in Ken's arms, her head resting against his shoulder.

"What are you thinking, Anna?" He whispered in her ear.

"I was just enjoying feeling close to you. I haven't seen much of you lately." She felt his body stiffen against her and regretted her words.

"Now what have I told you about complaining?"

"I know. I'm sorry. It just slipped out."

He pulled away from her, cupped her face in his hands, and stared into her eyes. One hand began caressing her cheek and ran through her hair, grasping a handful tightly which caused her to wince. He loosened his grip on her hair.

"Come," he whispered, taking her hand and leading her into the bedroom.

* * *

The next morning Anna opened the door to the balcony and drew in a deep breath of fresh air. The sun felt good as it warmed the pink satin nightgown she wore. Aware of Ken behind her, Anna sighed. His hands massaged her neck and shoulders. With the familiarity of a long-time lover, he slid his arms around her; his hands caressed her. His body lent its warmth to hers, and she leaned against him, sighing with contentment. At the feel of his breath on her neck Anna pushed her body even closer against him. His lips brushed behind her ear, and a shiver went through her body.

"Ken, you can't possibly—"

"Why not?" He laughed, his arms dropping from around her before he walked back into the bedroom. The large room, with walls of antique white, had a king-sized bed centered against one wall. A large walk-in closet opened on the left of the bed, and double doors on the right led into the large bathroom. Honey-yellow drapes flowed to the floor on each side of the sliding doors which led onto the balcony. She followed Ken across the pale gold, medium-pile carpeting.

"Don't ever underestimate me." One eyebrow lifted, and he grinned. "You know I can and will if I want to." He picked up his clothes from the chair.

"You're a devil," she said, taunting him. Anna sat on the side of the bed, leaning back on her hands. She pulled one leg up, allowing her nightgown to slide up her leg. Pouty lips teased him as she admired his lean body until it disappeared into the bathroom. He wore nothing but a pair of silk navy boxers. His voice, his laughter, his body, his touch, and his eyes—all these things totally mesmerized her. He knew her weakness for him and used it. "I know very well that you are capable of making love all night," she called out. "You're merciless."

His laughter teased her, and she loved it. In fact there wasn't anything she didn't love about this man. For a moment she lost herself in her thoughts and allowed the passion she felt at the beginning of their relationship to surge through her. But the unspoken truth was that the passion between them appeared to be waning. She wasn't sure just why, but his demands of her physically were becoming less frequent. There were no signs that there was someone else and yet she wondered. His mind appeared to be more on business than pleasure. *I know everything is all right with us. It's got to be.* She shifted her body and listened to the singing that came from the bathroom. *I'm pretty certain there's no one else. Or am I?*

As Anna perched on the edge of the bed and listened to the sound of the water running, she smiled, imagining the droplets running down his lean body. He excited her, and she enjoyed the feel of his body next to hers. The sound of water spraying ceased, and she heard the shower door open. Rising from the bed, she picked up the soft yellow comforter from the floor where it slid off the bed during their lovemaking.

Ken came out of the bathroom fresh from his shower, his hair still glistening with moisture, and put on his suit pants and shirt. He sank down on the side of the bed and reached for his shoes and socks. "I need you to do a favor for me."

"Okay." She sighed inwardly, picked up his jacket from the chair and held it to her face. His smell lingered on it, a masculine, spicy fragrance. A muffled thud startled her and caused her to look down. A .38 Special lay at her feet. She knew it was a .38 Special because her dad had owned one just like it. A cop for 35 years, he had insisted she learn how to shoot it. She leaned down and picked it up. The gun felt cold and heavy in her hand. It was sobering, and the warm feeling she had felt left her.

"What is this, Ken?"

"Nothing. I always carry a gun. Personal protection."

"Oh, of course." Uncertainty edged her voice.

"Now back to the favor I need." He got up and took the gun from her.

She made herself comfortable on the edge of the bed and waited for her instructions. She was used to the occasional request. They did not occur often and were never complicated.

He pulled a thick envelope from his pocket and gave it to her. "I need you to take this to 139 Duncan Avenue. Leave it with the receptionist at the desk and tell her it's for Anthony. She will know what to do with it. Do it tonight but don't deliver it before seven."

"That late?"

He leaned over and gave her a lingering kiss. "Yes, silly, don't whine, just do it." Looking in the mirror, he knotted his tie, straightening it with meticulous care.

She turned the envelope over in her hand, a frown on her face. "What is it, Ken?"

"Not necessary for you to know."

"It's bulky."

"Don't be too nosy. I might have to kill you." He laughed. "Just teasing."

She stared at him intently and didn't return his laughter. Somehow she felt he wasn't joking.

"Hey! I'm just teasing," he repeated.

"Okay, okay, I'll do it, but it will be dark by then. That's not what you would call a safe part of town, you know."

"I said don't whine. Just do it. Take your cell phone with you and call me if you have any problems. You'll be all right." He took her by both hands and lifted her from the bed. Strong arms wrapped around her and pressed her body against his. He kissed her with the familiar hunger that had aroused desire for him so many times before, and her concerns receded to the back of her mind.

I can't believe how easily he makes me respond to him. She sighed and, for a moment, allowed herself to enjoy his touch; then she giggled when she felt more than just a touch. Ken pushed her away.

"You vixen. Look what you do to me." Ken winked and smiled. "I must go. No more seducing, woman."

Anna liked the way he made her feel sexy and desirable, something no one else had ever done. "Oh, all right. If you must."

"Don't forget. Seven o'clock."

His reminder caused her smile to slip. "I won't forget. I'll do it." She handed him his jacket and opened the door.

He slipped on the jacket, leaned over, and gave her a quick kiss. Without a smile, he looked down at her. His eyes held a deep seriousness that made her feel uncomfortable.

"I know you will," he said. "I know you will."

Anna stared at the closed door. *Oh, God, what is he getting me into?*

* * *

Strong hands grabbed Anna from behind. The light aroma of a man's cologne filled her nostrils as a strong square hand slid around her waist, holding her against an unseen body. Another hand covered her mouth just as she opened it to scream.

"Be quiet," he whispered close to her ear.

She struggled against him, panic rising with the lump in her throat. She grabbed his arm and dug her fingernails into flesh. Her strength pulled against his, but she couldn't free herself of his grip. The muscular arm held her with little effort. She attempted to take a deep breath, and his fingers slipped between her teeth.

"Don't you dare bite me!" The man said as he pulled her head back against his chest.

"Listen, if you'll please be quiet, I'll take my hand off your mouth. You scream, and we're both dead. You hear me?" He waited a moment for her response.

She stopped struggling and shook her head.

He eased his hand from her mouth but kept it close, ready to muffle her scream if needed. Anna took a slow deep breath. His free hand fumbled in his pants while the other maintained a firm grip on her.

Oh, my gosh! He's going to rape me. Once again she struggled to escape, but he brought his free arm around her, capturing her against him.

"Be still," he said in a low voice. "Now look in my hand."

She squinted against the dim light rendered by a streetlight. His hand held something shiny, but she had difficulty seeing what it was. With his back against the building, he held his hand closer to her face. Then she saw it: a police badge. His grip relaxed.

"Now will you listen to me?"

Anna moved her head forward, resigned to his control, and felt his arms fall from around her body. She whirled around and faced the unknown man.

A dark, unruly curl fell over his forehead. Although not much taller than she, his muscular body gave the impression he towered above her. Dark piercing eyes stared at her. She felt exposed and vulnerable under his gaze.

"What are you doing here? Don't you know this is a dangerous part of town after dark? Hell, lady, it's dangerous in the daylight."

"I, uh, was delivering something for a friend and, uh, got lost."

"Delivering something?" His eyes narrowed warily.

"Yes, for a friend. Then my car broke down, and I didn't know what to do. I was trying to find help."

"This time of night? In this neighborhood? You've got to be kidding."

"Well, no, I'm not kidding." Anna nibbled on the side of her lip.

"Do you know how bad this neighborhood is, lady?"

"I –"

He put his hand over her mouth and pulled her further into the darkness of the alley. She heard the sound of distant voices drawing closer.

"Sh-h-h," he said. He shoved her behind him, listened, then turned to her and motioned for her to get behind a big trash bin.

She crouched in the darkness and waited, afraid the approaching men could hear her heart pound. She heard the tinkling of glass against the pavement, and the smell of cigarette smoke wafted through the air.

"Hey, man, what's up?" Laughter.

"Nothin, man, just hangin," the voice of the man who had grabbed her answered.

Anna eased to the corner of the trash bin and carefully peered around it at the entrance of the alley. Three men gathered in a circle in front of the cop who had pulled her into the alley, their voices a low rumble, followed by laughter. She watched the cop remove his wallet from a pocket and take out what looked like a lot of bills. He handed the money to one of the men. When the man reached to take it, the light from the streetlamp revealed his face. She was struck by the sharpness of his features. He glanced in her direction, and she quickly pulled back behind the trash bin. The low rumble of their voices didn't allow her to hear what they said. Every now and then she heard laughter. She eased to the edge of the bin hoping to hear more and slowly looked around the corner of the bin, holding her breath in anticipation. The sharp-featured man turned away, and when he turned back, he had something in his hand which he gave to the policeman.

"That's good stuff, man. Can't get crack like that on just any street corner, ya know." He raised his raspy voice to an audible level.

"Yeah," the policeman said, "it better be top quality. Cost enough."

Oh God, what have I gotten myself into? No, Ken, it's your fault. Suspicions rose in her mind, and Anna tried to control the fear beating in her veins. *I thought you loved me. You wouldn't put me in this situation if you did.*

More laughter and the men walked on down the street. The policeman lit a cigarette and leaned against the building and watched them. Once their voices faded he turned and walked toward her.

"You can come out now," he said in a low voice. He held a hand toward her.

She placed her hand in his, and he pulled her up from her crouched position.

"Lady, you didn't see a thing tonight, and I'd advise you not to come back to this neighborhood."

"But my car—"

"Your car? Oh, yes, your car. Tell you what, is it locked up?"

"Yes."

"Then I'll take you home, and tomorrow you can get a tow truck to come and pick it up, that is, if it hasn't been stripped by then." The man gave a low laugh.

"That isn't funny," Anna snapped.

"No, ma'am, it isn't, but it's a fact." He took her arm and led her to an old dark blue Chevy, its sides covered in rusted dents.

She stopped when she saw the car and pulled away from him.

"Is this your car?"

"Yes, it is."

"But I thought..." Her voice faded.

"It's the car I use on the job, and, no, it's not an official police car."

"Why do you drive this one?" She wrinkled her nose in distaste.

"You ask too many questions. Now, get in, please. We need to get out of here."

"I don't know about this."

"Well, let me put it to you this way. You can either get in and let me drive you home where you'll be safe or I can leave you here. I promise you, you won't be safe in this neighborhood by yourself."

Without further hesitation she got into the car, a look of disgust on her face. He grinned as he slid behind the steering wheel.

"What's your name?" He asked.

"Anna. I live on Taylors Drive, by the way."

"Oh-h, rich side of town, huh?"

"Not exactly."

"Well, ma'am, it ain't cheap living in that neighborhood. Whadda ya do for a living?"

She ignored his question and asked, "What's your name? I know your occupation."

"Do you now?"

"Yes, you're a cop on the streets looking for drugs. Now whether it's for yourself or your job is another thing, but that's your business.

He glanced toward her, grinned, but made no comment.

"What's your name?" Anna said after a moment of uncomfortable silence.

"John Mentz – Detective John Mentz."

She glanced out of the corner of her eyes. "Why don't you wear a uniform, Detective Mentz?"

"Because it would be unwise for me to wear a uniform." He coughed to cover a laugh that she heard anyway.

"Why?"

"You're joking, right? You really didn't understand what just happened in that alley, did you?" Anna heard him mutter under his breath, "She can't be that dumb."

Deciding to ignore the aside remark, Anna answered, "Well, not entirely, but I might have a gist of what was going on."

"I've been working that case for a month, and when I finally get them to complete the deal, you come along, lady, and damn near ruined it. You could've gotten us both killed."

"Deal? What deal?"

"Drugs."

"What? Are you kidding me?"

"I never kid."

"You're an undercover cop?"

John heaved a sigh. "Yeah, and wearing a uniform would rather, umm, well, not work under the circumstances."

Anna felt her face burn. "I … I guess I wasn't …" She paused. "Not my brightest moment."

He pulled the car up to the curb in front of her apartment building and turned the motor off. Anna watched him shake his head as he stared out the windshield. A soundless whistle blew air through his pursed lips before he turned to face her.

"You would be wise to forget about what happened tonight and keep your mouth shut about what you saw. Forget it ever happened. Seriously, lady, don't go back to that neighborhood again. You might not be so lucky next time."

"It'll be difficult to forget, but I'll keep my mouth shut. I promise you that."

"Good!"

Anna stepped from the car and watched as he drove away. "No, definitely not my brightest moment," she told the vanishing tail lights before she turned toward her apartment. "And certainly not Ken's either. How could he?"

* * *

"Something about that woman bothers me," John mumbled to himself. He pulled his car to the side of the road and pulled his phone out. He dialed a number and waited.

"Yeah, I need you to run a license plate for me. It's TLR463. Sure, I'll wait." He drummed his fingers on the steering wheel while he waited. It took several minutes, but the information was given to him.

"You're kidding. Damn!" He paused. "Okay, thanks." He hung up.

"No wonder she lived in that neighborhood," he said out loud. "She's Senator Levall's mistress." He gave a low whistle. "Hmmmm...I wonder what she was doing in that neighborhood at night?"

He started his car and pulled into traffic.

Chapter 3

The next morning Anna rose early. The telephone rang as she stepped from the shower.

"Hello," she said.

"Good morning, Anna."

"Ken. You're calling early."

"Is that a problem?"

"Well, no, of course not." She pulled the towel closer around her body. "What do you want?"

"Did you deliver the package?"

"Yes, but don't ask me to go there again."

"Why? Surely you can handle a simple chore like that."

"Don't talk down to me like that, Ken," she said in an irritated voice, "and thanks for being so concerned about me."

"You're acting like a child, Anna."

Her eyes narrowed and her jaw clinched. "My car broke down, Ken. I was stranded in a dangerous drug-infested neighborhood, and you tell me I'm acting like a child." Her voice rose shrilly.

"Calm down. You're evidently okay now."

"I was scared shitless, Ken. I'm not going back there." She caught a glimpse of her face in a mirror and was surprised at how pale and haggard she looked.

"You'll do whatever I tell you and no questions asked." He seldom used that steel edge when he talked to her.

"What?" Anna's eyes widened and her stomach clinched into knots.

"You heard me." He hung up the phone.

Anna turned off her portable phone and eased herself onto the side of the bed.

Damn him, he doesn't care. He has no concern for my welfare, or he wouldn't have said that. Her fist slammed into the mattress. *I thought he cared, loved me. Ha!*

As she dressed, the events of the night before ran over and over in her mind. *How could he? If not for a stranger …* She shook her head. *No, don't go there. Just calm down and forget about him for right now. I have things to do, better get with it. Hair appointment first. That'll make me feel better.*

With traffic, the trip to the salon would take at least twenty minutes. She grabbed her purse, made sure her cell phone was in it, and started out the door. The phone rang again. With a sigh, she turned to answer it.

I don't have time, she thought before she heard the answering machine click on. *Good! They can just leave a message.*

The fact that she was a few minutes late didn't matter. Andre′ was putting the finishing touches on the blond in his chair. Relieved, Anna grabbed a magazine and found a chair while she waited. Her cell phone rang. She sighed and answered it. It was her sister calling.

She closed her eyes and pictured Tina four years her junior, a college graduate with no major ambitions in life. Content to work as a librarian, Tina spent her spare time with volunteer work. Small built with brown eyes and hair, she attracted the attention of any man who caught her eye. *That's my little sister.*

"Hi, there," Anna said into the phone.

"Hey, where are you?" Tina asked.

"André's."

"How about lunch when you get through there?"

"Sure."

"I've something to tell you." Excitement tinged Tina's voice.

"Oh? What is it?"

"I'll tell you at lunch."

"Okay." Anna laughed. "Sounds like a new man in your life."

"We'll discuss it when I see you."

"Well, okay. Guess I can wait. What time and where?"

"One o'clock at Kelsey's, okay?"

"That's perfect. See you there."

* * *

"Anna, come, my dear, let's make you beautiful." Andre′ waved her to his chair. "How are you today, dear?" Tall and lanky, Andre′, a natural blond with crystal blue eyes, appeared to look straight through a person. The way he cocked his head slightly to the side and gave a quick and flirtatious smile charmed women. However, Andre′ had no interest in women.

She slid into his chair and watched in the mirror as his long slender fingers ran through her hair.

"I'm fine," she said. "Make me beautiful, Andre′. I need something to make me feel better."

"Oh, my, what's the matter?" He held up one hand. "Wait, let's get you shampooed. Then you can tell me all about it." He quickly lathered her hair and rinsed with water warmed to perfection, careful not to splatter anything but her hair. After wrapping a towel around her head, he ushered her to his booth and allowed the damp towel to drop to her shoulders. He ran a brush through her thick hair and proceeded to tell her about his week. She tuned out his constant chatter and just enjoyed the attention.

"Now tell Andre′ all about it." His voice broke through her thoughts and brought her attention back to the present.

"It's my sister, Andre′. She doesn't approve of my … my friend."

"Ah, Anna, you should follow your heart, but be sure. If you love him, go with what makes you happy …" The man shrugged. "But be sure he's worth your love."

"It's just that …"

"What, Anna? Do you have doubts? Is that what's bothering you?"

Anna looked at Andre′ in the mirror. He glanced up, their eyes meeting, and held her gaze for a moment.

"What doubts are you having, Anna? That you love him or that he loves you?" He smiled knowingly at her.

"He's a very important man, Andre′."

"Even important men need love."

"It's not about love. My sister believes he's into drug trafficking, and she's determined to prove it." Anna closed her eyes, remembering Ken's callused treatment the night before and this morning. She opened her eyes to search the ones in the mirror.

"That could be dangerous." He shrugged again. "Well, then if she can't prove it, she'll feel better about your relationship with him. But if she does prove it ..." he cocked his head and raised his eyebrows at her.

Anna lowered her eyes, a thoughtful look on her face. She sat quietly while Andre′ chattered constantly, intuitively not requiring any responses from her.

With an elaborate swirling of his hands, Andre′ announced, "You are beautiful! Just as I promised. My best work of all times."

"Yes, Andre′, it is, as usual, your best work." She smiled back at him, an uneasy reserve beneath her smile.

"Enjoy your lunch and give Tina my regards." He brushed a hair from her shoulder.

"Andre′?"

"Yes?"

"What did you mean when you said that could be dangerous?"

He didn't answer her. His smile faded into a worried frown.

"Are you the one who's been filling Tina's head with all these doubts?" Her voice gently prodded even as it accused.

"You might be wise to listen to your sister, Anna." The raspy harshness of his voice surprised her, and it took a moment for what he said to sink in.

"What do you mean by that?" she asked.

"Nothing, Anna. Don't pay me any attention. I'm in a funky mood is all. Enjoy your lunch." He turned abruptly away, dismissing her.

She picked up her purse, put some money on the counter, and, without a glance at Andre′, left the salon. She hurried to her apartment for a quick change of clothes. Feeling rushed irritated her, but hair coifed, dressed in a red linen suit, she walked into Kelsey's Bar and Grill at two minutes before one.

"You amaze me," Tina said as Anna dropped into her chair.

"Why is that?" Anna flashed her sister a quick smile.

"You are always dressed to perfection, hair in place, and on time. What a change in you."

"I guess Ken has been good for me in some ways."

"In some ways, I suppose, but in other ways he hasn't."

"Don't start that again, Tina."

"Aw, Anna, please listen to me. He's no good. Leave him. You just don't know the things I've heard about him." Tina reached over and grabbed Anna's hand.

"It's all gossip. I'm not listening to it. When you can find solid proof that he's a crook, I'll listen. Until then, forget it."

"Then I will. Just wait, you'll see."

The waiter arrived at the table and took their order, giving Anna an opportunity to change the subject of their conversation.

"Well, now, tell me what, or should I say who, this something is that you want to tell me about," Anna said in an attempt to turn the conversation away from herself.

"He's absolutely scrumptious, Anna. He's tall, blond, sexy sky-blue eyes, and built like a body builder." Excitement filled Tina's voice as a glow spread across her face.

"Wow, he does sound delicious."

Tina laughed. "You make him sound like a Popsicle."

"Where did you meet him?" Anna smiled at her sister's humor.

"He came in the library where I work. We got to talking. He kept coming back, and we just got to know one another."

"Have you been out with him, yet?"

"Oh, yes, many lunches, dinner dates, and movies that somehow we didn't see." Tina laughed.

"That's a good start. I'm proud for you."

"Thanks. I just hope you can meet someone decent and get away from that ogre you're involved with now."

"Tina, please." She pulled her hand back and glared at her sister.

"Anna, what is it that makes you hang onto him like this? Is it love?"

"You know why." Anna shrugged and lowered her gaze to her hands clasped in her lap. "I suppose I do love him in a way."

"It doesn't sound like it to me. You deserve better, Anna. No, we need to talk about this. I need to understand why you're so loyal to this man." Tina waited for a response from her sister, but when none came, she continued. "Please make me understand. Please."

"I never wanted you to know. I've always tried to protect you ever since Mom died." Anna looked up at her sister with eyes pleading for understanding.

"I'm an adult now. Quit trying to protect me."

"Well, after Mom died, I found out Dad had canceled the life insurance on Mom. Not only that, he left a lot of debt and Mom just added to it. You'd not quite finished high school and expected to go to college." Anna couldn't meet her sister's steady gaze, so she looked across the restaurant at the other customers.

"Go on." Tina said quietly.

"Somehow I managed, but in your first year of college everything just collapsed around me. As you know, I lost my business. What you don't know is I lost everything else, too. I ended up on the street, scared and not even with enough money in my pocket to get something to eat much less a place to live. I was worried sick about how I was going to pay for your next semester let alone books and the money you expected me to give you to live on." Anna shook her head, lips trembling.

"Anyway, a friend of mine happened to see me, and she stopped to talk. I couldn't help it. I broke down and told her everything. She took me to her apartment to stay with her until I could figure out what to do next. She was the one who took me to the party where I met Ken. I admit I was a bit over-awed with him, and it was next to impossible to turn down his proposition, considering I had you to take care of and get through school. So you see, I owe this man more than you can ever imagine." Anna stopped and took a deep breath.

"I'm so sorry, Anna. I had no idea."

"No, you didn't, and I preferred to keep it that way, but you just wouldn't leave it alone. So now you know."

"It's all my fault. I'm so very sorry, Anna."

"No, it wasn't your fault. Don't ever think that way."

"Okay," Tina said in a low voice.

"Anyway, I've got what I want."

"You've got Dad."

"What?" Anna frowned at her sister. "What do you mean?"

"You've got a man just like Dad. He's arrogant and controlling."

"That's nonsense. Where in the world did you get that idea?"

"Think about it, Anna. Dad was all military. Stiff, totally by the book. He ruled us the way he ruled the men under his command."

"Ken is not military."

"No, but he's arrogant, and he controls you. He expects you to jump at his every command." Tina took Anna's hand in hers again. "And you do it, Anna, you do it, don't you see? Just like you always did with Dad."

Anna looked at Tina and saw the pleading in her eyes.

"I really don't want to talk about this right now, Tina. Please, let's just enjoy our lunch."

The conversation dwindled as they waited for their lunch to be served. When the waiter left the table, Tina sighed.

"You took over when Dad died of cancer and Mom...well, Mom just went into her shell until she also finally died. You had to take care of Mom for the next year. I know it fell on your shoulders to take care of me also, and I will always appreciate the way you worked so hard, put me through college, gave me a home. You're a strong person, Anna. You can make it on your own. I just know you can." Tina paused. Her voice softened as she said, "I love you, Anna. You're the best sister a person could ever have. Just remember that."

Anna smiled at her. Staying mad at Tina for very long was impossible.

"I know, but I can't judge him on rumors or gossip. That's not fair to him. He's been so good to me. Don't you think I owe him the benefit of the doubt?" In her mind a little voice whispered, *Trying to convince Tina or yourself?*

"You don't owe him anything, Anna, but I do owe you."

"I owe him everything. He saved my life." There was a hint of bitterness in her voice. She bowed her head over her plate in dismissal. They ate in silence for a few moments, each lost in her own thoughts. Small talk filled the time while they finished their lunch, but Anna couldn't shake her resentment at Tina's interference in her life. And André's words kept playing through her mind. Tension built as she thought of the recent events, her sister's concerns, and the things Andre' said. *I do owe Ken so much. I have to give him my loyalty.*

As they left the restaurant, Tina turned to Anna, sorrow in her eyes and voice. "I'm sorry," she said, "I didn't mean to come on so strong. It ruined our lunch, and I wanted us to enjoy it."

"No problem." Anna kissed her sister on the cheek and gave her a hug. "Give me a call sometime, and we'll meet for lunch again."

"I will." Tina waved as she got into her car.

"And I want to meet this fantastic man of yours."

"You betcha." Tina said and threw Anna a kiss as she sped away.

Anna watched Tina's car pull into traffic. A dark green sedan pulled into the street behind her. Something, Anna wasn't sure what, made her watch the two cars as they made their way down the street, weaving in and out between the vehicles traveling in the same direction. The green sedan seemed to stick rather close to Tina's car. An uncomfortable feeling nagged at Anna, but she shoved it to the back of her mind when she opened her car door.

Her hand still on the car door, she paused. The feeling that someone other than herself had been in the car sent a chill through her. She quickly searched the front and back seats but could not see anything out of place. She slid into the driver's seat and turned the key in the ignition. As Anna pulled into traffic, a glance in her rearview mirror revealed a black sedan with dark tinted windows behind her. The car followed her out of the parking lot and stayed close to her as she drove down the road. Traffic was light. Fear and nausea filled her as her sweaty palms tightened around the steering wheel. Her foot stomped on the gas pedal, and she switched lanes without signaling. The car stayed right on her car's tail. She whipped in front of a gray Honda to her right, not leaving room for the black car to follow. The squealing of brakes behind her went unnoticed. At the next light, she made a quick right turn and watched in her rearview mirror as the black sedan turned onto the same street.

A constricting lump formed in Anna's throat and clammy hands shook. She took a hard left onto Duncan Boulevard, wheels screeching, and pressed her foot on the accelerator as she glanced in her rear view mirror again. The street behind her was quiet, no other car to be seen. Shaking, she drove the rest of the way home and breathed a sigh of relief as her car turned into the garage.

Her car pulled into its familiar parking space as automatically as a homing pigeon returns home. A click of the remote and her car was locked. As Anna scurried to her apartment, her heart rate did not slow until the door closed behind her and she turned the deadbolt. She ran to the window, pulled the curtain out of her way, and looked at the street below. A black sedan slowly drove past her apartment building. It was impossible to see who occupied the car because of the tinted windows, but she was sure it was the same car.

She fell onto the sofa, laid her head back, closed her eyes, and took slow deep breaths until the weak, shaky feeling eased. Her mind, however, did not.

Okay, calm down and don't make a mountain out of a molehill. First, you don't really know for a fact that car was following you. It probably was just a coincidence. Secondly, even if they were, they may not have meant any harm. They could just be watching you. So, silly, just chill and quit making this into something it's not.

Anna got up and went into the kitchen, a small room with hardwood floors, walls painted pale blue, and glass-front cabinets painted white. She took down a long-stemmed wine glass, opened a bottle of Riesling wine, and filled the glass halfway. Taking a sip of the pale amber liquid, she closed her eyes and felt the wine slide down her throat. A few more sips and her anxiety lessened.

Still feeling a bit restless, she set her wine glass on the cherry wood coffee table, slipped her shoes off, and allowed her bare feet to sink into the sandy-colored carpet. She sat on the plush Charleston-style sofa, covered in a gold and green paisley. Unable to sit, she stood up and paced around the room, her mind playing through the events of the day. She walked to the bookcase and ran her fingers lightly across the books, then moved to the green chair. She stopped, leaned over the table by the chair, and put her hand on the phone. She quickly pulled it back.

I don't know what to do. Who do I call? Should I tell what has happened? She moved to the window and carefully pulled aside the curtain. Her gaze swept up and down the street. All seemed quiet. *And would they believe me?*

The phone rang, breaking the silence. Startled, her body gave a jerk. She grabbed the phone.

"Hello."

"Hi, it's Tina. I forgot to tell you that I've got a new job."

"Oh, okay." She hoped Tina didn't notice the slight tremor in her voice.

"Are you all right?"

"Yes, yes, I'm fine. What is this new job?"

"It's with a research team, doing research." Tina laughed.

"That's great, Tina. I'm happy for you." There was a slight quiver in Anna's voice.

"You don't sound okay, Anna. Did that man hurt you?"

"No!" Anna replied much too quickly. "No, not at all."

"Well, I hope you're telling the truth, because if he ever hurts you …" Tina left the rest of her thought unsaid.

"I'm fine. Honest."

"I guess I have to accept that."

"Congratulations on your new job, Tina." Anna decided to change the subject.

"Thanks. This is what I've been waiting for. I'm so excited."

"Tina?"

"Yes?"

"Take care of yourself."

"I always do, Anna." Tina gave a small laugh.

"And be very careful."

Silence.

"I will be." Tina said in a puzzled voice. "Are you sure everything is all right with you?"

"Yes," Anna replied. "I love you."

"Love you, too. Gotta run now."

Anna hung up the phone, curled up on the sofa, and pulled an afghan over her. Her eyes closed in exhaustion.

A few moments later her eyes flew open, and she sucked air deeply into her lungs. *I'm suffocating! Can't breathe!* She quickly leaned forward and covered her face with her hands. In quick motion, she jumped up and started pacing the floor, fighting the fear that wanted to explode inside of her. *You've got to stop this! You've got to face your demons.*

She went to the window and eased back the curtain. Looking toward the street, she gasped in horror when she saw a black car parked across the street. Anna quickly dropped the curtain and backed away from the window. She quickly turned off the lights and found solace in the darkness that crowded around her. Anna's chest tightened, and the suffocating feeling returned. She curled into a ball on the sofa and pulled the afghan all the way to her chin. There she waited through the night, cringing at every creak of the walls around her.

Chapter 4

Traffic was heavy, but Tina maneuvered it skillfully. A frown on her face, she managed to keep her concentration on what she was doing. She noticed the dark green sedan behind her when she left the restaurant the night before, and it was obvious Anna had seen the car follow her out of the parking lot. Tina caught a quick glimpse of the worried look on her sister's face, and it bothered her.

The mysterious car followed her most of the way home, but she had made several sudden turns and eventually managed to lose it. When she got home, she locked all the doors and windows. Despite all her efforts, the night was long and mostly sleepless. However, it provided time to do a lot of thinking, and that brought her to a decision she hoped she would not regret.

The next morning doubts began to nag at her. Nagged at her a lot. She couldn't just do nothing. Out of exasperation she got in her car and pulled into traffic.

It was hard to keep her mind on traffic. She kept going over the things Anna had told her. The more she thought about it the more upset she became. A fast food store on the right caught her eye. It did not appear too busy, so she pulled in and went inside. After a few minutes, she brought her bottled water out to the car and slid in behind the wheel. Unscrewing the top, she took a big sip of the cold liquid. It felt good and helped clear her head.

"Jeez, I need to calm down and think," she said to the empty seat beside her. She took another sip of the cold drink and leaned back in the car seat. Eyes closed, she was unaware of the dark green sedan parked not far from her.

She raised her head and slammed her fist on the seat beside her. "I can't believe it. It's entirely my fault she's with that man. My fault!" She took another sip from the bottle and hit her fist against the steering wheel. The anger and need to do something built inside of her.

"It's up to me to do something about it, but what? Most of all, to pay her back. Dammit, I've got to do something." She finished her water and threw it in the nearby trash can. "I think I've got it. I know what to do now. I don't know whether to believe that proof exists or not, but I'll find out." Carefully pulling into traffic, she drove with deliberate movement through the heavy traffic, the dark green sedan barely able to keep up with her.

Her hand felt around on the seat beside her. When she finally found her cell phone, Tina dialed a number. It rang several times before a voice answered.

"Hi," she said. "I need your help with something." She paused and listened to the voice on the other end of the line.

"Please," she said, her voice pleading, "this really is important. Do you remember the other day telling me about a videotape you had that showed Senator Levall talking to one of his thugs about a drug deal?" She listened again.

"Do you still have that tape? I need it. I'll pay you whatever you want." The person on the other end of the phone spoke again, and a glint came into her eyes, a smile flickered on her lips.

"Okay, that's satisfactory. I'll get the money and be there in an hour." She turned off the phone and laid it on the seat beside her.

* * *

The neighborhood was old and rundown. It was late afternoon when she pulled up in front of a house that was one of the worse looking on that street. The windows were dark, and Tina hesitated a moment before getting the nerve up to get out and go to the door. She didn't like being here but was determined to go through with it. Taking a deep breath in, she knocked on the door and tapped her foot nervously while she waited. After a moment, she knocked again, more firmly and louder. The door opened immediately, and she found herself staring at a tall, thin man with a mustache and steel-gray eyes.

"Whadda ya want?" The man said curtly.

"I, uh, I need some information. I was told you could help me." She was trying to keep her composure, but it was hard. Her impulse was to turn and run, but she stood her ground.

"Oh? Who sent you here?"

"A mutual friend. Ike Peterson. He said you'd help me." She looked at him with pleading eyes. "I really do need your help. Please."

He seemed to hesitate, then opened the door wider and stepped to the side for her to enter. Tina reluctantly stepped in the doorway and walked into the living room. Looking around, it was a sparsely furnished room with stained carpet and grimy, torn curtains on the windows.

"Sit," he said, pointing to a dingy sofa against a dirty wall.

She sat on the edge of the sofa and waited while the man lit a cigarette. He glanced out of the side of his eyes at her and sat in a chair across from her.

"Now how can I help you?" He asked.

"I need proof that Senator Ken Levall is running a drug ring."

"Hold on there." He held his hands up as if to ward her off. "Are you with the police?"

"No! You see, my sister is involved with the senator. I'm trying to get her to leave him. She doesn't believe he is into the drug scene. She told me she wouldn't leave him unless I show her proof."

"And what makes you think I have proof?"

"Ike told me you have some tapes showing the senator making some drug deals."

"Wait a minute, girl." He was shaking his head. "I can't give you anything like that."

"But I've got to have it."

"Not from me, you don't." He gave a half-grunt, half laugh.

Tina looked at him thoughtfully. "All right. Have it your way. But I was prepared to pay $10,000 for just one lousy tape." She smiled. "Obviously you're not interested." Tina stood up as if to leave.

The man quickly held up his hand, a wicked glint in his eyes. "Now don't go rushing off, lady."

"Oh, but you let me know you weren't interested, so there really isn't a reason for me to stick around."

"Well, we may be able to come to an agreeable understanding."

"Oh, really?"

"Yeah."

Tina sat back down and waited.

"You, uh, said something about $10,000."

"Yep," she said, "I did." She silently prayed he wouldn't see the desperation on her face and up the price.

He was quiet for a moment, his fingers picking at the frayed threads of the chair he sat in. Finally he seemed to get his nerve up. "I might be willing to sell it to you for $10,000."

"You might?"

"Okay, I will," he said quickly, "I will."

"Then we have a deal. Right?"

"Right." His eyes watched hungrily as Tina opened her purse, pulled out a large wad of money. He reached out to grab the money from her, but she pulled her hand with the money back and out of his reach.

He looked at her in surprise. "Hey!"

"You'll get your money when I get the tape, and I want to view it to make sure it's what I want."

He frowned in disappointment but left the room. When he reappeared a few minutes later, he held a videotape in his hand. Placing it in the player, he sat back while Tina watched the tape. When it was finished, he took the tape out and laid it down on the table beside her.

"Okay," she said and handed him the money.

Tina had been in the house for an hour when she came out with the videotape in her hand, got into her car, and drove away.

There was no one around to appreciate the smile on her face.

Chapter 5

The next morning was a busy one at the boutique. Lisa Taylor had only worked there for the past month, but she took care of the customers with ease, leaving Anna free to restock and do her monthly inventory for reorders.

"Lisa, there should be a new shipment coming in today. Let me know if it does." Anna said.

"Yes, ma'am, I will." Lisa continued straightening displays.

"You haven't been taking your full lunch hour. Why don't you take some extra time today?"

Lisa, surprised, looked at Anna. "Oh, thank you, I will."

"I know you think I haven't noticed, but I have." Anna gave a small laugh. "I'm sorry I've been so preoccupied lately."

Lisa smiled and shrugged. "Oh, that's okay. I know you had a lot on your mind. I just tried to take up as much of the slack as possible."

"You've been doing a good job, Lisa. I appreciate that."

"Thanks. I've tried hard. I like working here."

"Good. Now get out of here and enjoy your lunch."

Lisa grabbed her purse and scurried out the door.

After Lisa left, silence settled over the store. Anna finished straightening the displays and began working on the monthly inventory. When the door opened, she looked up. A customer stood at the counter, one tall, blond, and very handsome man. He smiled at her.

"May I help you?" Anna smiled back.

"I'm sure you can." His blue eyes bore into her, exploring her from head to toe, a smile playing with the corners of his mouth.

"Well, uh, how may I be of help?" She felt a flush of red creep up her neck into her face.

"I'm looking for a sexy nightgown for a very special lady."

"Okay. If you will just follow me, please." She led him to a rack of gowns. "What size?"

"Oh." He looked thoughtful and said, "Well, I don't know, but she's about your size."

"I see." Anna pulled out several gowns for him to examine and spread them on the counter. "Look at these. If you don't see anything here, I have more."

While he thumbed through the gowns, she picked out a few more for his consideration.

"Is this gift for a special occasion or just to impress her?" Anna said.

"Oh, I guess more to impress her."

"I see."

"I'm not good at this," he admitted. He looked at the line of gowns Anna had spread across the counter. "Which one would you choose?"

Anna picked up a red floor length gown with lacy roses covering the bodice. "This is beautiful." She held it against her body.

"Yes, it is."

Something in his voice prompted her to glance up. The look in his eyes made her uncomfortable, and she quickly laid the gown down. She could feel the warm flush working its way up her neck and into her face. Averting her eyes, she busied her fingers with the lingerie.

"Red is your color," he said.

"Uh, I take it you like this one?"

"Yes, I'll take it."

"Cash or charge?" A quick completion of this sale was obvious in her demeanor, she feared, but the man did not appear to notice it.

He pulled a large wad of bills out of his wallet, looked at her with a lop-sided grin on his face, and raised an eyebrow.

She placed the gown in a gold box, rang up the sale, and silently breathed a sigh of relief that this man would soon be on his way out the door.

"What is your name?" He made no move to leave.

"Uh, Anna."

"That's a beautiful name."

"Thanks."

"My name is Carl."

"Nice to meet you." She picked up the inventory.

"Do you live close by?"

"No." Anna felt uneasy and glanced toward the door, silently praying someone else would come in the shop.

"Oh, okay."

"Well, you have a good day," she said, hoping he would take the hint.

He picked up his package, smiled at her, and said, "You do the same. Maybe we'll meet again."

Anna gave a weak smile and shivered as she watched him leave.

* * *

Lisa came back from lunch earlier than expected.

"Whew! Am I glad to see you!" Anna told her.

"I know you said I could take a longer lunch, but I just didn't have anything to do. I'd rather work." Lisa looked at Anna's pale drawn face. "Are you okay?"

"I'm okay, but I'm glad you came back when you did."

"Why? Was something wrong?"

"Not really. It's just that last customer made me feel uncomfortable. He was asking some personal questions."

"Oh-h-h. I should've been here."

"He didn't touch me, but he sure gave me a look. You know, the kind that makes you feel they're undressing you."

"Yeah, I know that look. You better be careful, Anna. He could be a stalker or a rapist."

"Oh, you bet your bottom dollar I'll be careful."

"Maybe I should just bring a sandwich and eat my lunch here for awhile, so you won't be alone."

"Thank you, Lisa, but I'll be all right. He probably won't ever come back. Anyway, you need to have that break away from work. Believe me, I've been taking care of myself for a long time. I'll be careful."

"Okay, but if you change your mind, let me know. I don't mind."

"I know, but I'll be fine, thanks. I'll be in my office for a short while." She gave Lisa a smile and squeezed her hand reassuringly.

Anna went to her office, leaving Lisa to handle the store. She picked up the phone and dialed a number she had dialed many times before.

"Hello?" Ken answered immediately.

"Hey."

"Anna?"

"Yes." There was a slight tremor to her voice.

"Are you okay?" He always seemed to know when something not of his making was wrong with her.

"I guess."

"You don't sound it."

"I, uh, just need to see you for a few minutes."

"Well, sure. I can take a lunch break in about 30 minutes."

"Okay, I'll pick up a couple of sandwiches and meet you at my apartment. Will that be okay with you?"

"Sure. That'll work."

Anna hung up the phone and grabbed her purse. As she went to the front of the store, she stopped. "Lisa, I'm going home for lunch. Will you be all right?"

"Sure, I have my pepper spray here if anyone should come in who looks suspicious. And if I see anyone hanging around outside, I'll lock the door and call the police."

"That will be fine, Lisa. Be watchful and don't hesitate to close the store if you feel uneasy about anything or anyone. I mean that, okay?"

"Will do."

Anna left the store and hurried home.

* * *

When she got to her apartment, the door stood open slightly. A small shiver of fear ran through her before the door swung all the way open. Ken stared at her from the doorway.

"Oh, thank goodness, it's you." She gave a sigh of relief.

"Who did you think it was? My God, Anna, you look like a scared rabbit."

"Well, the door was ajar, and I knew I hadn't left it like that. I wasn't sure who was in there."

"You knew I'd be here. Hey, what's wrong with you?" He pulled her inside the apartment, helped her remove her coat, slipped his arms around her, and held her trembling body in his arms. "You're shaking. Tell me what has you upset so much."

"It's been one of those days. A strange man came into the store today. I just hope Lisa is okay by herself there. Then finding my front door ajar when I got here ...well, it kind of scared me."

"She'll be fine, I'm sure," Ken said. "And I don't think you have anything to worry about. I was the one who left your door open." A sheepish grin crossed his face. "I'm sorry. I really didn't realize I'd not closed it behind me. So you see, everything's fine. Just calm down." He took her arm and pulled her to the sofa. "Come on, sit down, and I'll fix lunch."

"Ohhh." She groaned, covering her face with her hands.

"What's the matter?"

"I was supposed to bring sandwiches. I forgot."

He laughed and shook his head at her. "Don't worry, I'll find something here." Ken set the table and heaped each plate with a ham, lettuce and tomato sandwich and chips. He poured iced water in the two glasses, then turned, and bowed.

"Lunch is served, my lady." He escorted her to the table, gave her shoulders a comforting squeeze, and seated himself across from her.

"If you don't mind, Ken, I need to get my mind on something else. Let's not talk about what happened this morning," Anna requested.

"That's fine. We'll just enjoy this gourmet meal I've fixed for us. We can talk afterward."

She smiled her relief. "Thanks, Ken, for being so understanding. Lunch looks good."

He attempted small talk, but Anna was not inclined to talk. The rest of the meal was eaten in silence. When they finished eating, Ken gathered the dirty dishes and put them in the sink.

"Come on. Let's sit on the sofa, and you can tell me all about it." He took her by the hand and led her to the sofa. "Feel better now that you've eaten something?"

"Yes, thanks." Moments like this, when he showed compassion, made her devoted to Ken. *Tina can't possibly be right about him*, she thought. *She's never seen this tender, caring side of him. Only I have. He doesn't show that side of himself to the public. It's all business with him. All business.* She gave a slight smile. *And he's had things on his mind. That's why he snapped at me, seemed not to care.*

"Now, tell me about this man, Anna."

"I guess I'm being silly, but ..."

"But?"

"Well, today at the boutique, this man came into the store. He was looking for a gift. Of course, I found one that he liked, but ..."

"Go on."

"He just made me feel uncomfortable, Ken. There was something about the way he looked at me that I didn't like."

Ken put his arms around her and hugged her. "Well, I doubt you'll ever see him again, Anna. I wouldn't think any more about him if I were you."

"You're probably right," Anna said, cuddling into his arms a little more. "He said his name was Carl."

"Carl?"

She felt his body stiffen against her, and his arms pulled slightly away from her.

"Yes, why?" She asked with a suspicion she hoped he would not notice.

"No reason." His tone of voice seemed distracted, and Anna glanced up at him. A scowl crossed his face.

"I've got to get back to work." He gave her a quick squeeze and rose.

"Is something wrong?"

"No, just something I need to look into."

"Oh, okay. I guess I should get back, too." Shocked by his sudden mood change, she didn't ask questions, just ducked her head and stood.

"It'll be okay, Anna." His voice softened. "Don't worry about it any more, okay?"

"Okay."

He kissed her on the nose, gave her shoulders a little squeeze, and walked to the door before he paused and turned back. A quick smile spread over his face. He blew her a kiss and disappeared, leaving Anna staring at a closed door.

Something's not right with this picture. He brushed the whole thing off as if it were nothing, but then at the mention of this Carl... She slowly picked up her coat and purse, her mind playing over the events that had just happened. *He knows something about it.* As quickly as she thought it, she dismissed it. *I'm imagining things, just my imagination.* She left the apartment unable to shake a growing uneasiness.

* * *

Ken sat at his desk, a frown on his face. After a moment, he picked up the phone and dialed.

"Karen, I don't want to be disturbed this afternoon, please." He listened and then said, "Thanks."

He dialed another number and waited for his call to be answered.

"Meet me at our usual place in twenty minutes. Don't be late."

The senator glared at nothing as he left his office. "I'll stop this," he muttered as he climbed into his car. "He had no right ... Nobody messes with what's mine."

Exactly twenty minutes later, Ken entered the park and sat down on a bench. Before long he heard a low whistle. He got up and strode to the closest grove of trees. As he stepped out of sight of the other people in the park, Carl grabbed his arm.

"What's up, Senator?" Carl asked in a low voice.

Ken spun around, rage etched deeply in his face.

"What the hell did you mean?" Ken's voice hard.

"Mean?" Carl chuckled. "By what?"

"You know what." Carl's flippancy angered Ken even more.

Carl shrugged. "Tina was so delicious I wanted to see what big sister was like. She's even more delicious."

"You're going to ruin the whole thing if you're not careful." Ken put the end of his finger against Carl's chest and looked him in the eyes. "And you *will* regret it if you do."

Carl seized Ken's finger and pushed it away.

"And that, my friend," Ken said through clenched teeth, "is a promise, not a threat."

Carl stared into Ken's eyes without blinking and said, "Oh, really?"

"This is the only time I'm going to say this. Stay away from Anna, her store, and her apartment." Ken turned and walked away.

Carl glared after the senator until he was out of sight.

"We'll see about that, Senator. Yeah, we'll see," he muttered to himself.

* * *

Anna locked and checked the doors of the apartment before she went to the garage. *Maybe I'm paranoid,* she thought as she scrutinized cars and shadows while she drove through the garage. All seemed to be okay; however, when she pulled into traffic, she watched for any vehicle which might be following her.

Not in the mood to go back to the store, she rode around and allowed her mind free run. *I'm losing my mind, must be. Ken is the same as he's always been. I'm imagining things ... got to be. He loves me, not owns me.* After a while, she went back to the store.

"Hi," Lisa said, looking at her dubiously. "Are you all right?"

"Yes, thanks, Lisa. I'm fine. I just had to think some things over, that's all." She smiled, hoping to reassure her assistant more than she herself felt.

"Good. I'm sure he won't be back, Anna, but just be careful."

"I will. Believe me, I will." Anna gave a wave of her hand and disappeared into her office.

Chapter 6

Tina glanced in her rear view mirror and pushed her foot on the accelerator to speed up her car. A black sedan with tinted windows was right on her. She shook her head in disbelief as the car behind her sped up also. A chill went through her, leaving her with a bad feeling. A very bad feeling.

She picked up her cell phone, not daring to pull over to the side of the road to make her call. Tina hit the speed dial that held her sister's number and waited to hear her sister's voice on the other end.

"Answer me, Anna. Please answer me." She gasped as she watched the car advance and nudge her bumper, giving her enough of a jolt to scare her.

A click on the other end of her phone brought her to attention. *No! No! Don't give me the answering machine. I need Anna.* But the recorded voice of her sister left its message, and the beep sounded.

"Anna, please, please call ASAP. I have something important to tell you." Hand shaking, she hung up and started to dial another number when the dark sedan bumped her again. This time a little harder, then it slowed down to allow space between the two cars. It whipped quickly around her and sped down the road, leaving her behind. Tina gave a big sigh of relief and set her phone down beside her.

"I don't know what that was about, but I'd bet it had to do with that videotape," she mumbled. "Maybe I should've given it to the media instead of Anna." She thought for a moment. "I don't know. I may have put Anna in danger by giving her that tape. Oh, God, what have I done? I have a feeling I don't have long to live. I just hope it doesn't mean trouble for Anna."

She wiped away the tears that had flowed onto her face. "Please, Anna, forgive me."

Chapter 7

At first Anna thought she dreamed the distant ringing of the telephone, but the sound became louder and more insistent, drawing her reluctantly out of a deep sleep. She glanced at the clock and groaned. Seven o'clock.

"Damn! Who could be calling so early?" The bed creaked as she rolled over and picked up the receiver. "Hello."

"Good morning." The deep voice brought her wide awake, and she sat up in bed.

"Yes? John?"

"That's me. How are you?"

"I'm fine."

"Thought I would check on you after the other night."

"Thanks for coming to my rescue."

"Sure. Just don't make a habit of it. I can't afford it."

"I'm sorry. I was in a strange neighborhood." Anna tried to smile but instead grimaced and was glad John couldn't see her. "Then my car broke down, and it scared me shitless, if you'll excuse my language, and I'm rambling."

"Yes, you are."

"I'm sorry." She felt like such an idiot.

"That's okay, just stay out of that neighborhood. It's not a good place to be in the daytime, much less at night, and a woman alone. You're lucky you didn't get killed, lady."

"I know that now. I don't plan on going back there."

"I'll take your word for it. Now, change of subject, I wondered if you had anything going on tonight?"

A surge of unexpected excitement jolted her. "I—uh—I'm not sure. Why?"

"I just thought maybe we could have dinner together. There's a real nice Italian restaurant on Desmond Avenue," John answered.

"Well, I don't know..." Her voice drifted into uncertainty. She didn't really know this man, and after the danger and experience the other night, she hesitated. *Why am I hesitating to say no? Ken ... Why am I tempted to say yes?*

"You do like Italian, don't you? If not, there are plenty of other places to eat." He paused before saying, "Of course, if you're not interested, that's okay." His voice cooled.

"Oh, no! It's not like that. I'm just not sure if I have tonight free."

Silence.

Was he thinking about it, or figuring a way to politely back out of his invitation?

"Surely you would know if you had other plans or not." Beneath the cold terseness of his voice lurked disappointment.

"Well, there are special circumstances that I can't discuss at this point, but I really would like to go out to dinner with you." She paused to take a breath. "Please, could I check and get back with you?" *Because, whether right or wrong, I really want to see you again.*

There was the soft raspy sound of breathing, then a sigh. "Sure. Just give me a call at 555-6773."

"Thanks, John, I'll be back in touch."

After hanging up the phone, she put on a pot of coffee. As she stared at the phone, she nibbled her bottom lip. "Okay, he doesn't own me, and he's not been acting like someone who loves me." She squared her shoulders, grabbed the phone, and placed a call to Ken.

"Hello." His deep voice seemed to growl.

Damn, she thought, *he's not in a good mood.*

"Hello," he repeated.

The agitation in his voice aggravated her, and she hung up without saying a word. "I don't know about this. Ken doesn't seem to be in a good mood," she mumbled as she moved away from the phone.

An hour later, after she showered and dressed, she dialed John's number. Her hand trembled a bit with nervousness.

"Hello?" he said.

"Hi, there."

"Anna?"

"Yes, it's me." She laughed.

"I hope you're calling to accept my invitation."

"Sure am."

"Good! I'll make the reservations. Pick you up around seven. Is that okay?"

"That'll be just fine. I'll look for you then."

"Great. See ya this evening."

"Okay."

The day passed quickly. Anna usually preferred closing the shop herself, but she passed that responsibility on to her assistant. She skillfully maneuvered her car through heavy traffic, and though her nerves screamed, she managed to walk in the door of her apartment in record time and sighed with relief. The day behind her and the thought of a date with a handsome man put a smile on her face.

"Damn! Who can this be?" she muttered when she saw the blinking message light on her answering machine. A sinking feeling centered in the pit of her stomach as she stared down at the blinking light for a moment before she pushed the button to play the messages, two of them.

The first message, timed at 3:45 p.m., was from her sister.

"Anna, please, please call me ASAP. I have something important to tell you."

"What now?" Anna muttered. "If it's so darn important, why didn't she call me at the store?"

The second message, timed at 4:00 p.m., was from Ken.

"Anna, give me a call when you get home. I'll be in the office until late tonight. I have a conference from seven to nine. Call before or after."

She picked up the phone and dialed Tina's number first. After a number of rings and no answer, she hung up. She had a moment of concern but knew that Tina often turned off her answering machine.

I'll try later, she thought. *It can't be that important. When I do talk to her, she's going to get a piece of my mind about not leaving that damn answering machine on. Ken can wait, too. He's probably forgotten he even called me.* She gave a half snort. *Besides, he needs to wait on me for a change, let him wonder what's happening.*

She left a trail of clothes as she made her way to the bathroom. Turning on the water to fill the tub, she tested the water for the proper temperature and sprinkled in some bath salts. When the tub was half full, she stepped in and sank into the warm water and bubbles. She closed her eyes and let the warmth soak into her body. Slowly the day's tension eased, and she felt rejuvenated. After being in a suit and high heels all day, the soaking bath made her feel like a new woman. She applied fresh make-up and put on a pink cotton dress with a soft white sweater. She gave one last look in the mirror before she turned off the lamp.

The doorbell rang. Opening the door, she stared at the handsome man before her. Dressed in a maroon open-neck knit shirt and navy pants, he, with his dark hair and piercing dark brown eyes, left her speechless. This was quite a different sight from the scruffy man the other night.

"Aren't you going to let me in?" John asked. "Or are you going to just stand there and stare at me?"

"Oh. Yes, of course, come on in." She stepped aside.

His eyes roamed over her from head to toe, openly appreciating her beauty. She ran her hand over the skirt of her dress, her tongue moistening her lips. She hadn't felt like a teenager on her first date in a long time.

"Hey," he said, "it's okay. I'm not here to arrest you, just to enjoy your company."

Her smile still held a hint of uneasy anticipation, but she found herself beginning to relax.

"What's the name of this restaurant?" She asked.

"Santino's."

"I've heard of it, supposed to be really good."

"Then let's go. Are you hungry?"

"Oh, yes." She gave a nervous laugh.

* * *

Low lights dimmed the restaurant, and soft romantic music flowed from unseen speakers. A mixture of tempting aromas assaulted their nostrils. The host greeted John like an old friend who frequented the restaurant often.

He certainly seems comfortable here, Anna thought. *I can't help but wonder ... oh, come on, it doesn't matter how many other women he's brought here. Just relax and enjoy yourself.*

"We have your table ready," the waiter said and led them to a table set away from the rest of the restaurant. There was a faint whiff of garlic as he leaned forward to seat her.

"I have the Brunello Di Monotalcino ready to serve as you requested." The waiter opened the bottle and poured John a small glass.

John twirled the wine in the glass, holding it to the light with an appreciative look. He closed his eyes and sniffed the wine before taking a sip, swirling it around in his mouth and swallowing it. He spoke to the waiter in Italian, then smiled his approval. The waiter filled both glasses, stepped back from the table, bowed, and retreated.

John smiled at Anna, picked up his glass, and held it up in a toast.

"To life," he said.

"To life." Anna took a small sip of the unfamiliar wine. "Oh, this is marvelous."

"Yes, it's an Italian wine. Very expensive but well worth it."

"You speak Italian?"

"Fluently. I was stationed in Italy when I was in the Army. I liked it so much I went back after I got out. Lived there for five years before returning to the States."

"If you liked it so much, why'd you come back?"

"There's no place like home." He grinned and picked up a toothpick, sticking it in his mouth.

"Are you ready to order?" The waiter interrupted.

John looked at her with a raised eyebrow.

"I don't know what I want," she said.

"Would you like for me to order for you?"

"Well ... sure. That would be nice."

John turned to the waiter and spoke in Italian again. That done, he turned back to her.

"Again tell me what you were you doing in that neighborhood the other night?" He asked.

She laughed, a twinkle in her eyes. "Oh, no, first you tell me what you ordered for me. For all I know I'll be eating eel or something else just as gross."

"What? Are you telling me you don't trust me?" With a fake frown, he looked at her with twinkling eyes as he removed the toothpick he had been speaking around.

She started to answer but hesitated. "We-e-ll, yes, I do trust you, but... oh, hell, I just want to know." She hiccupped.

John laughed so hard Anna thought he was going to lose his breath. She waited until he stopped laughing and, with another hiccup, said, "Well?"

He took another toothpick and put it in his mouth while she wriggled impatiently in her seat. "I think you'll like it," he said. "Eggplant parmigiana is one of their specialties."

"Mmmm, that's a favorite of mine." Anna raised her glass. "You know, this wine really is excellent." She took a big sip. "I do love a good wine."

He didn't answer her, and when she looked at him, he gazed at her with eyes full of desire. She held her wine glass up and waited for him to touch his glass to hers.

"To beauty," he said.

"To dessert," she returned in a slurred voice. *Whew, this wine must be potent.*

"You're already thinking about dessert?" He laughed.

"Oh, yes. What are we having for dessert?"

"I can't believe you. Well, if you really think you can hold it..." He reached for a menu from the waiter's cart. "How about a chocolate cherry cake with drippings of yummy chocolate syrup?"

"That sounds absolutely scrumptious."

"Good. I'm glad you're satisfied. Now, I got your message, and I agree. We won't talk about the other night. Let's concentrate on each other instead."

She raised her eyebrows and took another sip of wine. Silently, she simply waited for what he would say next as her thoughts churned. *This is going too fast. What's wrong with me? How can I suddenly be so interested in another man?*

"Okay, how about telling me a little bit about you."

"Well," she said," I was born in Charleston, South Carolina, and raised all over the place. I have one sister who is a few years younger than I am. Our childhoods weren't exactly normal, mine especially, since I was the older."

"Why is that?"

"We were army brats and moved around a good bit. I didn't have many friends as a child because of that." She shrugged and remained quiet for a moment, lost in thought. Then she said, "When I was about three weeks from graduating college, my Dad died of cancer after a long illness. Mom just lost herself in another world. The medical bills were tremendous. Tina, my sister, was about a month from graduating high school. She took it really hard. I guess she figured she would never be able to go on to college, and to her that meant the end of her life. Anyway, Mom lived for a year after Dad's death. It was left up to me to take care of her, pay the bills, and get Tina into college. There wasn't much money left for any of that."

The waiter rolled his cart to the table and served their salads. He gave them a fresh bottle of wine and also refreshed their glasses. While he did that, Anna leaned back in her chair and took the opportunity to survey the room. John's eyes never left her face. Finished with her survey of the room, her eyes swung around to meet his. She smiled at him.

"Let's eat," she said. "It sure looks good."

"Dig in!" He smiled back at her and picked up his fork.

There were a few moments of silence while they ate their salads. When John took a sip of his wine, which resulted in a loud slurp, Anna couldn't help but giggle.

"I'm sorry," he said, embarrassed at his breach of etiquette.

"Oh, that's okay. It kind of helps break the ice, if you know what I mean."

He laughed so loud it caused some at surrounding tables to turn and look in their direction. "I getcha. So-o-o, continue your story. Did your sister have to go to work in a slave factory or not?"

"Of course not! There wasn't much money left by the time I paid the bills and buried my Dad, but I managed to find a job at a large department store here in Daylan and managed their clothing department. It took me a while, but I worked my way up to a buyer. After about a year of working as a buyer, I managed to save enough to start my own business. It was hard to do since I had Tina to take care of, but somehow I did it. Looking back to those days, I don't know if I could do it again. Anyhow, I paid for Tina's way through college and did my best to support her while she went to school and saw to it that Mom was taken care of. I practically lived on bread and water those four years." Anna gave a small laugh.

"Gosh, didn't your sister work and help some with the expenses?"

"Well, yes, she tried to do her part, summer jobs, working during the holidays and breaks. About the time she found a job after graduating and got on her feet, I lost my business. I couldn't find another one and was on the brink of losing everything." She brushed a wayward curl from her face, exposing the soft creamy skin of her cheek. "I, uh, I really don't want to remember that time."

"Why didn't Tina help you out?" He licked his lips while he watched her slender fingers twirl that wayward curl around her fingers.

Anna shrugged one shoulder. "I didn't tell her. She was still trying to get on her feet and trying to create her own life. I didn't want to add to that struggle." She stared at the table. "It wasn't easy, and I was really despondent. So I went to a party with Jean and met the senator." She glanced at John through her lashes and shrugged. "He… he made me feel like I was the only woman in the room." She sighed. "You probably won't understand this part. Sometimes I don't."

With another slight shrug, she added, "I know it sounds silly, but he was a real charmer. Anyway, we got to talking, and I told him something about my predicament. He took me back to my friend's place after the party, and I gave him my phone number. He did call a few days later and offered to help me. I guess I felt I didn't have much choice." Anna straightened her back and lifted her chin. "I did what I thought I had to. It was the only option I had at that time."

"I see." John gave a silent whistle before he gave her a slight grin. "I, uh, I don't need details. If he offered to help, I'm sure, well…" This time he shrugged.

"He's been good to me, and, and we loved each other," she said rather defensively. *Loved? Where did that come from?* She shook her head. She sighed again and looked straight into his eyes. "Now tell me about you."

"Me? Not much to say. I was born in Dallas, Texas. Two brothers. We all went to college, and I decided to get into police work. One brother became a boring accountant and the other a cattle rancher. My parents died of natural causes about two years apart. That's about it."

"Have you ever been married?"

"I, uh, was married for about two years. She couldn't take being a cop's wife."

"I'm sorry," she said. "Any children?"

"No, I wanted them, but she didn't. I guess it's a good thing we didn't have any."

He changed the subject to a lighter and livelier subject, and Anna found herself laughing more and more. The evening passed quickly.

John opened the car door for her. Before getting in, she turned to him and smiled.

"It has been a wonderful evening," she said. "Thank you."

"Your company has been very enjoyable," he replied formally before smiling. "I'm the one who should be thanking you."

"I do have one complaint, though."

The smile left his face and his forehead furrowed into a frown.

"What?" He asked. "Please tell me."

"The evening went by much too fast. I don't like it ending so soon." She giggled. "I need a chance to find myself again, I guess." She giggled again. "I've been lost way too long and am rather confused."

Relief smoothed the furrows in his brow, and he laughed. "Then we shall do it again if you like."

"Oh, I like."

The drive to her place was made in a comfortable silence. John turned into the entrance of her apartment building and pulled up to the front door. He left the motor running and turned to her with a smile.

"You didn't invite me, but I'm not going to come up to your apartment."

"No, I didn't invite you." She laughed. "You did rescue me, but after all, I really don't know you yet, and despite appearances, I'm really not that kind of a person."

"I never said you were, and even if you didn't invite me tonight, you will. Guess I don't get a kiss either, huh?"

"But it's just the first date."

He reached his arms out, gathered her into his arms, and pulled her to him. His lips caressed hers with a gentle longing before he leaned back and smiled at her.

"Now go, woman, get to bed. I know you're tired, and I have work to do. Do you want me to walk you to the door?"

"No," she said, "but thanks, I'll be fine." She heard the longing in her voice and hoped it wasn't too obvious to him.

He leaned toward her, his lips barely brushed hers. She closed her eyes and enjoyed the moment as his gentle kisses made their way to her ear and down her neck.

"Goodnight, pretty lady," he whispered in her ear.

She opened her eyes and saw the desire etched deeply in his face and eyes. She drew away from him. "Goodnight," she said as she stepped out of the car. Leaning forward so she could see him, she added, "Thanks for a very lovely evening." She shut the car door and watched him drive away. As she turned toward her door, her thoughts whirled. *Talk about being mixed up, I certainly am. How can I love one man and be so interested in another?* She shook her head as she used her key to unlock the front door. *I don't think I'm that kind of person … I don't think.*

Chapter 8

The next morning Tina burst through the door to Senator Levall's office and didn't stop until she reached his desk. She put both hands on the desk and leaned over it. Their eyes met, his hard and icy, hers blazing with anger.

"I believe I told my secretary I didn't want to see you," he said icily.

"You did, but I wasn't going to let that stop me." Her voice quivered with hate and determination.

He sighed and laid his pen down. The senator leaned back in his chair and waited. Tina paced back and forth in front of his desk, tightened jaw working furiously. He waited. After a few minutes, Tina stopped her pacing and turned to face him.

"I don't know any other way to tell you this, so I'll just say it the way I feel it. I want you to leave my sister alone, and I want you to leave her out of your drug business," she announced.

He leaned forward with hands clasped on top of the desk and smiled sarcastically at her.

"First of all," he said, "I don't have a drug business. Secondly, it's Anna's choice to be with me, and thirdly, just who are you to demand anything of me?"

"Oh, come off it, you arrogant son of a bitch. I'm not an idiot. I have proof that you run a drug business."

"What proof could you possibly have?" He demanded as he stood and glared at her.

"I-I have it, but you'll never get your hands on it. I have it in a safe place." She back away from her position in front of his desk.

"Yeah?" The senator laughed. He looked at her with disdain and said, "Wouldn't be a videotape, would it?"

"H-how did you know?"

Without answering, he walked around the desk with long deliberate strides. She pulled further away from him as he reached for her. Moving quickly to the side, she turned toward the door.

"Come here, you little..."

She reached the door and opened it. Turning to look triumphantly at him, she smiled. "I mean it, Senator, leave Anna alone and out of your crummy business or I'll send that video to the proper people." With that she slipped through the door and gave the senator's secretary a salute before disappearing down the hallway. His secretary turned and looked at him with questioning eyes. He closed his office door, giving her no opportunity to ask those questions.

* * *

Senator Levall dialed the phone and waited impatiently while it rang. Lips pressed together, he drummed his fingers impatiently on the desk listening to ring after ring.

"Come on. Answer the damn phone," he said. After a few minutes, he hung up and dialed another number. Someone answered on the second ring.

"Yes, I need you to take care of a problem. I'll meet you in fifteen minutes at Preston Park." He hung up the phone, gave his secretary some instructions, and left the office.

The senator pulled his jacket closer around him. There was a slight nip in the air, but the sun was warming. Early spring rejuvenated most people, but the senator had his mind on other things. The quiet park held a few mothers pushing bundled-up babies in strollers. He let his gaze roam around the park as he paced close to a wooded area.

"My, my, aren't we impatient," a deep voice drawled.

The senator whirled around and stared coldly at the man who had come up behind him. "It took you long enough. I've been waiting for quite a while."

"All of ten minutes. Calm down, Senator, and let's talk." Carl Blakely grinned and lit a cigarette.

"We have trouble brewing."

"Trouble?"

"Yes, Anna's sister paid me a visit. She claims to have proof of my little side business. A videotape. I think she's about to make life difficult for me."

"Trouble can be fixed. No problem. I was wondering when you were going to get around to letting me handle this little problem for you. After all, she's why you hired me." Carl threw his cigarette on the ground and rubbed it out with his shoe. He turned to leave, but the senator grabbed him by the arm and pulled him back around.

"Yeah, well, it's time to do it. I want it done now. Permanently. I want the problem solved once and for all." The senator's eyes glazed over, and his hand tightened on Carl's arm. "And get the video. I want it." His fingers dug in even harder. "Stay away from Anna, you hear me?"

Carl grabbed and removed the senator's hand from his arm. He winked, gave a thumb's up, and disappeared into the woods.

The senator gave a sigh of relief, straightened his jacket, and walked nonchalantly back to his car.

* * *

Anna flinched as she ripped the tape off a box. Lisa was helping a customer while Anna opened the boxes of new stock.

"Drat it," she said under her breath, looking at the nail she broke. "So much for that manicure. Might as well have saved my money."

The bell over the door tinkled. Anna assumed it was Lisa's customer leaving and turned to ask Lisa to help her. Instead she found herself face to face with her sister. Tina's face was drawn, her eyes red and swollen.

"Tina! What's wrong?" Anna pulled her sister into her arms. After a brief hug, she said, "Come on. Into my office with you. I'll get us a cup of coffee." She ushered Tina into the office and closed the door once Tina was inside.

Anna turned back to tell her assistant, "Lisa, I'm going to be tied up with my sister for a bit. She looks horrible. I don't know what's wrong, but something is. Please, unless you can't help it, don't disturb us."

"Sure, go ahead. I'll handle things out here."

"Thanks, Lisa, I appreciate it. Sorry for leaving you with this mess."

Lisa waved her away, so Anna poured two cups of coffee and put some cookies on a plate. She went back to her office and handed Tina a cup, set the other cup on her desk with the plate in the middle. She sat down and looked at Tina. Taking a sip of coffee, she waited.

Tina sat with her head down, rolling the stirrer through the coffee. The silence lay heavy around them.

"The coffee's pretty good," Anna said, pushing the plate of cookies toward Tina. "Try a cookie with it."

Tina shook her head at the offer of a cookie, but she took a sip of her coffee.

"Well, then, want to talk about it?" Anna prodded.

Tina took another sip of coffee, leaned back, and sighed deeply. She looked at Anna and said, "Yes, I think I better." She looked at her hands holding the cup for a moment then looked up at Anna. "I have something I need you to keep for me. It needs to be locked up where no one can get to it."

Curious, Anna leaned forward, resting her arms on her desk, fingers lightly intertwined. She frowned at Tina, concern growing inside of her. "I can do that for you, but Tina, what is it?"

"I... I don't think you need to know that information—for your own safety."

"What do you mean?"

Tina put her coffee cup down and pulled a VCR tape out of her purse. She handed it to Anna and stood up. "Look, don't ask questions. Just put this up—no, lock it up. Don't show it to anyone, ya hear? Don't even tell anyone that you have it. And if—if anything happens..." she swallowed, "to me, give this to someone you can trust in the police department, but be sure you can trust that person, very sure."

"Okay. I know someone, name's John." Anna took the tape, opened her safe under her desk, and put the tape in it. "It'll be safe in here, but Tina, are you okay?" Anna turned back to find she was talking to an empty room. She got up and quickly ran into the store. Through the front window, she saw Tina get into her car. Anna ran to the door, but Tina's blue Corolla slid into traffic. Anna watched as a dark sedan pulled behind Tina's car and followed her.

"Oh, God, Tina, be careful." A weight filled her chest. "Be safe," she whispered.

Chapter 9

In the dark apartment, Anna could see the flashing red light on the answering machine. Flipping on the light, she pressed the message button.

"Anna, where are you?" Tina's voice, shrill and breathless, reverberated from the tape. "I need to talk to you ASAP. It's important. I should have told you already. I should have told you today when I saw you, but I didn't think you'd believe me. You need to know what Ken is into. He's trouble, Anna. Please call me." There was a loud noise in the background, and the message ended.

"What the ..."

The machine started playing the second message, from Ken.

"Where the hell are you, Anna? I told you to call me. Are you ignoring me? That would not be advisable. Call me as soon as you get in."

She erased the messages and dialed Tina's number. The phone rang several times.

"Hello," Tina said.

"Hey, what's up?"

There was silence at the other end of the telephone.

"Tina?"

"I—I can't talk right now."

"But you said it was important." *This is odd, doesn't make sense.*

"I know. I'll call you later." Click.

For a moment Anna stood there with the phone in her hand. *What is going on? Maybe I should go over there? But, but she said she'd call me later.* She hung up the phone, in a quandary about what to do.

* * *

Tina hung up the phone and stared at the two men standing in front of her. The tallest one grinned at her, revealing a missing tooth in front. His hand held a 9mm Glock pointed at her. The shorter man stood slightly behind the man with the gun. He stared at her with cold eyes that left her chilled with fear.

"Who are you?" Her voice rose to a hysterical shrill.

"Hee, hee." The taller man gave a silly laugh. "That's none of your business, Missy."

She looked from one man to the other and back to the taller man, her eyes wide with fear. "How did you get into my apartment?"

"You idiotic woman. You shouldn't leave your front door unlocked. That's an invitation for bad people to come in."

"What do you want?" She heard the slight tremor in her voice but hoped he didn't notice it.

"You know what we want." The tall guy said in a gruff voice, waving the gun around.

"No, I don't know." She did but wasn't about to admit it to him.

"I think you do, bitch," the shorter man said.

"Honest, I don't," she said, hoping she sounded sincere.

The man with the gun stepped toward her. She cringed, a gasp escaping her lips. He stopped, cold eyes piercing through her. He stood there for a moment, then turned to the shorter man.

"Search this place, and I mean don't leave a corner unturned," he said.

Tina watched as the man searched her apartment and wondered what they were going to do when they didn't find the videotape. Without looking at the man holding the gun on her, she could feel his eyes on her.

"Hey," he called out, "how're ya doing in there? Found anything?"

"Not yet. Still looking," the shorter man called back.

The tall man motioned to her to sit down. Tina sat on the edge of the sofa, her body stiff as if poised for flight.

"Ya know, we've been watching you for a while." He laughed. "Yup, the senator has plans for you. It upset him a lot when you kept nosing into his business. Then when he heard you got that videotape, well, that was the last straw for him."

"I don't know what you're talking about. I don't have a videotape." Despite the fear that gripped her, she looked at him with hatred.

"Yeah, sure."

"Why were you watching me?"

"The senator wanted you watched. He didn't trust you. Guess he was right about that." He shook his head and looked at her with disgust. "You shudda left it alone, ya know. All that pushy ta do about the senator running a drug ring. Wasn't none of your business. Don't pay to butt into other people's business, ya know."

The shorter man appeared in the doorway which led to the bedroom.

"Did ya find it?" The taller man turned his attention to the shorter one.

"No. I've torn this place apart, and there's nothing." He looked around the living room. "Guess I could look around this room." He raised his eyebrows at his cohort as if asking permission.

"Go for it."

Tina winced as the man began the search of her living room, aware that the man with the gun was still watching her.

It didn't take long for short man to search that room. When he was through, he turned to the other man and said, "Nothing here either. Maybe she doesn't have it, Boss, like she said."

"Nah, she's got it somewhere. Just not here." The man with the gun walked over to her, grabbed her arm, and jerked her up from her seat. "Ya gonna tell me what you did with it, girlie." This was a statement rather than a question.

She looked up at his bloodshot eyes. There was a line of perspiration beading along his upper lip, lips pressed into a thin line of frustration and impatience. She had a feeling he was working hard to suppress his building anger. A shiver of fear went through her.

"What do you want me to do now, Boss?" The short man said in a quiet voice, waiting for the man with the gun to give him direction. The taller man stood silent, holding the gun pointed at her.

Tina watched as his fingers played with the trigger of the gun, her body tensed as she waited for the inevitable. Her mind raced with thoughts of what she could do to get out of this situation but knowing she was completely helpless and at this man's mercy.

He slowly lowered the gun, and she closed her eyes tight in relief, letting out a long breath she did not realize she was holding.

"You little bitch," he said in a voice filled with bitterness. "You may think you've won, but you'll get yours. And soon, too." He motioned to the shorter man, and they left, not bothering to shut the door behind them.

Tina ran and shut the door, locking it. Her body began to shake as she leaned against the door. After a moment, she went to the window and looked out. The two men got in a green sedan and drove away, their tail lights disappearing onto the night. Then she pulled the drapes closed, leaving her head against the curtained window, willing her heart to stop beating so fast. She knew it would, and she knew when.

* * *

A couple of hours later the doorbell rang, interrupting her thoughts and delaying any action. Anna checked the peephole and opened the door.

"Come..."

"Where the hell have you been?" Ken lashed out at her, his eyes steel sharp and cold with anger.

"As I was saying, come in." She opened the door wider and stepped aside.

He stepped into the apartment, and when she had shut the door, he turned and brought the back of his hand across her face.

The force slammed her back against the door. Stunned, she reached up and touched her mouth. Blood covered her fingers where his ring had slashed her lower lip.

"Where have you been?" He repeated. "You never called the other night, not a word since."

Anna shivered, but she stood straight. "Don't ever hit me again. I mean that."

"Answer me."

"Why? You don't have the right to question my actions." She frowned before adding, "But, I went out to dinner with a friend."

"I left you a message to call me. Why didn't you?"

"I just got your message," she lied, "and was getting ready to call you when you rang the doorbell. No point then when I could talk to you face to face."

He turned away from her and in a low voice said, "Who was your friend?"

Anna shrugged. "Oh. Well, he was the policeman who so graciously rescued me the other night." She closed her eyes as she fingered her lip. *I don't know this person. Has he been there all the time?*

"Rescued you?"

"Yes, when I got lost in that neighborhood where you sent me and my car broke down. You do remember that, don't you?" Sarcasm dripped from her voice.

He turned around and looked her in the eyes.

"Why didn't you call me?"

"I, uh, I forgot my cell phone."

"Stupid bitch," the senator snarled.

"How dare you. I should've had my phone with me, yes, but I didn't, okay?" Her voice grew icy. "That doesn't give you the right to call me names or hit me."

"It just seems to me you make a habit of forgetting your phone." He reached for her, but she moved out of his grasp. Anger covered his face, but his eyes revealed pain. He moved toward her quickly, grabbed her arm before she could get away, and pulled her to him. A strong hand tightly grasped her arm, and Anna winced in pain.

"Anna." His voice dropped to a low moan. He pulled her to him and pressed his lips against hers with a longing hunger. "Oh, Anna, I'm so sorry."

"Leave me alone," she said through clenched teeth, pushing him away from her. Her eyes blazed with anger. "I will *not* explain to you again why I did what I did. And don't expect me, much less tell me, to make any *deliveries* for you again."

"Anna, calm down."

"And," she shrieked, "don't you ever... hit me... again."

"Please, Anna, calm down. You won't be making any more deliveries for me. I promise."

"And never ever call me stupid bitch again."

He half turned away from her but stopped. Sighing he turned back to her, a look of defeat on his face, shoulders slightly slumped forward. "I apologize for that. I, of all people, know that you are not stupid. Anna, if you will just listen to me, you'll realize I'm trying very hard to apologize. You know I'm a hot head, but I do love you." His voice softened, and he reached for her, pulled her against him, and tenderly kissed her.

Anna closed her eyes and tried to struggle. He worked the magic on her body, as he knew how, the tension in her body slowly eased, and she soon leaned into him, wrapping her arms around his neck. For a moment she forgot her anger and allowed the passion he created to surge through her body. *He does love me. He does. And … and I love him. I do. Surely I do. Don't I?*

His arms tightened around her, his lips lingering against hers, careful not to hurt her injured mouth.

"Anna, Anna. Am I losing you?" He whispered close to her ear.

She swallowed and tried to smile. "No. No, of course not. Why would you say that?"

"Because…"

"Because?"

"I don't know. Just a feeling."

"I'm the one who should wonder, Ken."

"Why do you say that?"

"You didn't care about my welfare the other night. I'm sorry to keep harping on it, but that's a dangerous neighborhood."

"You were fine. It's not my fault you didn't carry your phone with you. If you had, you could've called me and would never have had to get out of your car."

Anna pushed away from him, her mouth open in disbelief.

"Aw, come on." Ken reached out to take her by the arm. "Get over it, will you? You owe me, and anyway, nothing happened to you, did it?"

"Owe you?" Her voice rose to a higher pitch. "Owe you?"

"All I've done for you over the past five years? Dammit, woman, yes, you owe me." His controlled voice held an edge of sarcasm.

"Well, I think you've been sufficiently paid back by now."

"Oh, the sex has been good, I admit." He grinned. "But I'm not through with you."

"Don't count on that."

Anna walked to the door and opened it. She stood with her hand on her hip waiting for him to leave.

He shook his head, threw up his hands in exasperation, and walked to the open door. He stopped when he reached her, leaned down to kiss her, but she turned her head away. His kiss landed on her cheek. The door closed firmly behind him as he exited the apartment.

* * *

Anna lowered herself onto the sofa and covered her face with her hands. Taking slow, deep breaths, she waited for her pounding heartbeat to slow.

I'm going crazy. I must be. I almost let him make love to me after ... She shook her head and muttered, "And I'm attracted to another man. I don't understand me. I don't understand ... I don't understand anything." When she felt composed again, she reached for the phone and dialed her sister's number.

"Dammit, Tina, what's up with you?" After several rings and no answer, Anna hung up. "I'll just go over there. Something's wrong. I just know it is."

The garage echoed with an eerie silence as she made her way to her car. With a short beep at the touch of the remote, the car door opened, and she slid behind the steering wheel. A shadow caught her eye, and she glanced into her rearview mirror. There was nothing there. Still she quickly locked her doors. Glancing around, she noticed a dark sedan with tinted windows parked in the row of cars behind her. About that time, her cell phone rang with a voice mail message.

"Hi, Anna, it's Tina. Sorry I haven't gotten back to you before now, but the love of my life has had me busy, if you know what I mean." Tina laughed. "I'll call you tomorrow, and maybe we can have lunch. Oh, I forgot, you have to see the beautiful gift he gave me. Love you." Then there was a click as the phone disconnected.

"Strange," Anna muttered, "she didn't mention what was so urgent. Maybe I should go over there anyway." She glanced at her watch and thought, *Twelve-twenty. Gosh, I didn't realize it was so late. Should I go or not?* Anna frowned. *She sounded okay, but what was so urgent when she called before?* She dialed Tina's number again, but still no one answered.

Puzzled and somewhat frustrated, she contemplated the dilemma a few more minutes before glancing in her rearview mirror at the black car parked across from her. The tinted glass made seeing into the vehicle impossible.

"I wonder what that car is doing there. I've never noticed it in this garage before." Anna strained to see if anyone was in the car but was unable, so she decided it must be empty. It took a moment longer before she placed her hand on the door handle of the car.

"Oh, well, guess whatever it was wasn't so important after all." Sighing, she gathered up the courage to get out of the car and return to her apartment.

* * *

Tina hung up the phone after leaving Anna a voicemail. Hopefully, that message will make Anna not worry about her. She hated lying like that to her sister, but it was better this way. At least she hoped so. Tina sat down on the edge of her bed and looked around at the mess her apartment was in. Unable to hold the tears back any longer, she buried her face in her hands and cried.

"My God, what have I got myself into? I really need to talk to Anna and try to get her to listen to me before it's too late for her, too." She lowered her hands, a heaviness in her chest, as it sank in what trouble she may have caused for her sister. "Oh, Anna, what have I done?"

Chapter 10

One…two…three… Anna counted the rings, her frustration mounting.

"Tina, answer the phone, dammit." Anna paced back and forth in front of her desk until someone knocked on the office door.

"Come in," she said as she hung up the phone. She glanced at her watch. Ten-thirty in the morning. Not even lunchtime. *It's going to be a long day,* she thought.

Lisa stuck her head through the door opening.

"You have a phone call on the other line," Lisa said.

"Thanks." Anna answered the other line with a curt, "Hello."

"My, my, are we not having a good day?" Ken's voice was teasing.

"Oh, hi, Ken. No, I'm afraid I'm not." The chill in her voice should have discouraged any more pleasantries.

"Surely you're not still mad at me. I'm sorry for being such a grouch the other night. It was a tough day at work that day, and things just weren't going well. Still I shouldn't have taken it out on you like that. Can you forgive me?"

She was silent, not sure of just how to answer. *How do I answer him? Do I remember the good times, the loving times, and forgive and forget? I don't know what to do, how I feel.* Anna took a deep breath, which she then exhaled.

"I, uh, guess so," she said.

"Guess?"

"I'm sorry, Ken, I just really can't think about it right now."

"What's the matter, Kitten?"

"I'm worried about Tina."

"What's the matter with Tina?"

"I don't know, just a feeling I have."

He laughed. "Well, I'm sure she can take care of herself, just like you. She's a strong and independent person. Have you heard from her?"

"Well, I had a voice mail from her several days ago. She said she'd been busy and she'd call me."

"Sounds as if she's okay then, so why are you so concerned?" Ken's voice sharpened.

"I don't know." She sighed. "I know it sounds silly, but it's just a feeling I have."

"You're right. It does sound silly. She's fine, Anna. Just relax and quit worrying so much."

"I suppose. She did sound okay." *But I'm not convinced. My gut feeling tells me something isn't right.*

"See there. You'll see I'm right."

"Yeah, I guess so. What did you want, Ken?"

"Nothing in particular. Just checking on you. Now relax, Anna. I'm sure Tina's fine. She's got a lot of you in her, you know, so have some faith in her. You worry too much."

Anna didn't say anything, but a worried frown creased her face. The silence grew.

"Well," he said, "guess I better get some work done."

"Ken?"

"Yeah?"

"Thanks." Her voice softened at his concern and encouragement.

"Anytime, Kitten."

She believed him.

* * *

Ken slowly placed the phone down, a worried look on his face. Dialing another number, he patiently waited for an answer on the other end.

"Is it done yet?" He said when the call was answered.

"Not yet, but it will be soon," the deep voice said.

"Make it real soon." Ken hung up the phone. The fingers of his right hand drummed on the desk as his mind worked with desperate intent. A few moments later he stood up, pushed his chair hard against the wall, and proceeded to pace.

"That little bitch," he muttered to himself. "That stupid little bitch. She'll be a dead bitch soon. It better be soon, real soon."

Ken sat down again and tried to occupy his mind with work, but the death of Tina did not stray far from his thoughts.

* * *

Anna hoped keeping busy would help get her mind off Tina. Still the day was long and never ending. That afternoon at four the phone rang.

"Yes, Lisa?" she asked into the phone.

"You have a call. Do you want to take it?"

"Who is it?"

"A gentleman. He said just to tell you his name is John, and you'd know."

"Oh, yes, I'll take that call."

"Okay, he's on line three."

"Thanks, Lisa." Anna pressed the blinking button on the phone. "Hello, John."

"How are you?"

"Not well, I'm afraid."

"Are you sick?"

She gave a small laugh. "No," she said, "I'm just worried about my sister. I can't seem to get in touch with her."

"What's up with your sister?" The concern in his voice stroked her ear.

"Well, she called me and left a message that she needed to talk to me about something urgent. I tried to call her back, but she didn't answer her phone. Her voice mail was evidently turned off. She does that sometimes, so I really didn't think too much of it being off—at the time."

"Why didn't you just go see her?"

"I was going to, even went so far as to get in my car, but I had a voice mail message on my cell phone from her that said she was okay. She had been with someone who was special in her life, and she sounded so happy. Anyway, it was really late so I went back to my apartment."

"So, I'm afraid I don't see the problem."

"I know it sounds silly, but I don't know. It's just a feeling I have. Maybe it's the fact that she did say she would call me later and she hasn't. I haven't been able to get in touch with her either." She sighed into the mouth piece. "I know you think I'm crazy, but I feel that something's not right. I can't shake it."

"Well, give her a little more time. Then if you don't hear from her, we'll get the police to check on it."

"Okay." *He's probably right, but how much time? Just when do I panic?*

"In the meantime, you need something to alleviate your mind. How about dinner tonight?"

Two men and so different. Why not? "Well, sure. What time?"

"Say sixish."

"No, that's a bit early if you don't mind. I've got a lot yet to do here, and I need time to change and freshen up."

"No problem, will seven be better?"

"That would be fine, thanks."

"All right, see ya then."

She hung up the phone, feeling better than she had all day. *I need to decide who I want in my life, and who not.* She sighed and then smiled as she considered the upcoming date with John. *I don't have to be afraid when I'm with him. I do like that.*

* * *

Anna put the last entry into her log book and filed the receipts for the day's sales. She slammed the file cabinet drawer shut and picked up her jacket and purse. For a brief moment she considered retrieving the tape Tina left with her and watching it. The phone rang, saving her from making a decision. She hesitated, not wanting to answer the call and be held up any longer.

Oh, heck, it may be John. Gosh, I hope he doesn't want to cancel. She put her purse and jacket on the desk and grabbed the phone.

"Hello."

"You sound breathless. What have you been up to?" Suspicion filled Ken's voice.

Oh, shit! "I was working on my books. I have some catching up to do."

"I see. Well, I thought I could spend some time with you tonight. Sound like fun?"

"Uh, I'm afraid it's not possible, Ken. Not tonight anyway."

"You can do books tomorrow, Anna."

"I'd rather do them tonight. I've found an error and want to get it solved now, or I may miss something."

Silence.

"I'm sorry, Ken," Anna said, forcing sincerity into her voice.

"You know, Anna, he's not worth it. He'll just drag you down to his level. Take my advice and don't go there." His voice hardened, yet she could hear a hint of pain beneath the coldness.

"I don't know what you're talking about, Ken."

"Oh, you know. You know very well what I'm talking about. Or should I say *who* I'm talking about."

"That's enough of that. I'll see you another night. Now I'll say goodbye." She hung up quickly before he had time to say anything more. Grabbing her jacket and purse, she locked up the store and left.

* * *

The doorbell rang. Anna finished clasping the dainty diamond heart pendant around her neck. She ran a well-manicured finger over the pendent and thought about the night Ken gave it to her. It had been one of their best of times, a party at the mayor's home. When he arrived to pick her up, he had flowers in one hand and the necklace in the other. A big smile on his face gave away the excitement he felt. Anna smiled at this memory, then she shoved it to the back of her mind. It was just a memory now. She gave herself a final once over in the mirror just as the doorbell rang again and hurried to open the door.

"Hi!" John smiled at her, the soft light of the hallway accentuating his olive complexion.

"What is this?" She laughed, pointing to his clothes.

"My working clothes."

"I thought we were going out to dinner?" Her smile faded.

"Well, we are… kinda." A mischievous glint appeared in his eyes.

"Kinda?"

"Wait, you'll see."

"Okay. Do I need to change my clothes to something more casual?"

"No, you're fine as you are." He bent down and picked up a small bag that was sitting out of her sight and shut the door behind him as he stepped into her apartment. He went to the phone and dialed a number. "We're ready here. Can you give me, say ... a half hour?" He hung up the phone and turned to her. "Mind if I use your bathroom?"

"Be my guest, but..."

He disappeared, shutting the bathroom door behind him.

"Well!" She huffed. Shaking her head, she turned on the stereo and soft music filled the room. She waited on the sofa, arms crossed. "I wonder what he's up to."

Twenty minutes later John came out, clean and dressed in a pair of dark green pants and a cream colored knit shirt. Anna smiled her approval as her eyes roamed admiringly over his body.

"All right, now what?" She asked.

"We wait."

"Wait? For what?" She tilted her head and raised one brow.

"You'll see." A big grin on his face, he cuddled beside her, his arm resting on the top of the sofa behind her. "Nice music. Sarah Brightman?"

"Yes."

"She's one of my favorites."

"Mine, too. But what does that have to ..."

The doorbell rang. John quickly rose and went to the door. He said something she couldn't understand and moved to the side. She gasped in surprise as two men in white jackets entered with a cart full of food, dishes and even a candelabra; the smell of pork and apples filtered through the air. John showed them to the kitchen, and they disappeared.

"The music will be perfect with our dinner plans," John said.

"Yes, it will be." Her eyes gleamed with pleasure as his plans crystallized in her mind. "By the way, what is the special occasion?"

He held out his hands and shrugged his shoulders. "Happy birthday?"

"But it's not my birthday." She laughed.

"It did put a smile on that pretty face of yours."

"Thank you for that. I needed it."

"I know. Shall we?"

Anna got up from the sofa and took his arm. He seated her at the dining table, and he sat across from her. One of the waiters poured a small amount of wine in John's glass and waited. John took a small sip and swirled it around in his mouth. After swallowing, he nodded his approval. The waiter filled both glasses while the second waiter proceeded to serve dinner.

John leaned forward and covered her hands with his. The candlelight reflected in his eyes, creating a sparkle that added to his charm.

"Are you enjoying this?" he asked.

"Yes, it's very nice. Thank you." She smiled softly.

"You're welcome. I just thought it would do you some good to get your mind off things for a little while and just relax and enjoy."

She took a small sip of wine.

"Mmmm, it's delicious. What is it?" Anna held the glass to the light and looked at nearly clear liquid.

"It's a Fume′ Blanc, a favorite white wine of mine. It goes well with pork loin."

She put her glass down as the waiters served dinner and smiled across the table at John. She hoped her face didn't reveal the heavy sadness she felt.

He smiled back at her and lifted his glass in a toast.

"To life, happiness, and success."

Anna touched her glass to his then put it to her lips, hesitating before drinking to the toast.

The dinner was delicious with soft music in the background, the conversation kept active by John's efforts. Anna remained quiet, unable to hide her preoccupation. When the couple finished dinner, the caterers packed up and left. John took her by the hand, led her to the sofa, and sat beside her.

"I'm trying," he said.

"I know. I'm sorry. I'm not doing well, am I?"

"What's wrong, Anna?" With one finger under her chin, John tipped her face toward him. "Talk to me."

Her mouth quivered as she choked back the tears.

"I don't know, John. I'm just confused and unsure about everything. My life seems to be falling apart, and I don't know what to do about it." Anna fought to control the tears. "I don't know what I want, where I went wrong. I thought I knew. I thought I knew ... before you came into my life." Her voice softened and faded as if in deep thought.

He slipped his arms around her and drew her against him. His lips smothered hers with kisses, and she responded with equal passion. Her hands explored his body hungrily, finding the growing bulge of his manhood. His response accelerated her desire as passion burst into open flames, burning out of control. She unbuttoned his shirt, ran her tongue down his neck, and nuzzled her nose in his chest hair. Gently she sucked each tiny nipple until they became hard and firm.

He ran his hands down her back, his breath coming quicker as her lips roamed down to his stomach. Her hand unzipped his pants. Her kisses did not stop until she reached the edge of the soft curls that crowned his manhood. She slowly stroked him as his hands fondled her buttocks, moving to her breasts. All of a sudden Anna felt his body stiffen, and he quickly pushed her away from him. He buttoned his shirt and zipped his pants, his hands trembling, a layer of perspiration on his forehead.

"What's wrong?" She looked at him, frowning, eyes wide and uncertain.

"I can't do this, I'm sorry."

"Why?"

"I—I just can't. Not like this."

"Did I do something wrong?"

"No, no, you didn't. It's just so animal-like. You know, no feeling, just pure lust."

"What do you want, John?"

A hint of a smile played on his lips, and his eyes softened as he gazed into her eyes.

"Romance," he whispered, "and love. You are doing this out of confusion and stress, maybe because that's what you expect I want. That's not right, Anna."

"I see." She turned her back to him, buttoned her blouse, and straightened her clothes. "As you wish, then."

"Anna?"

"Yes?" She kept her back to him.

"When this is ended—and I mean if it is, all this, uh, relationship with you and the senator—well, then we'll see." He ran his fingers through his hair. "I have to admit what you told me the other night, and the impression you left, bothered me." John touched her shoulder. "I don't share well, Anna, and I want more than physical, umm, release."

"I know. My life is a mess. I need to straighten it out, get rid of..." Her voice faltered. "I made a big mistake, but I did love him at first." Anna shook her head. "I still care for him in a way. I can't help it, but ... but he's changed ... and what I feel ... I need to get away from him, need to do something." She covered her face with trembling hands.

John exhaled a deep breath. "I shouldn't say anything, but that may be sooner than you think."

She turned to face him, a puzzled expression on her face. "What do you mean?"

"Just be patient and see what happens." John hesitated. "You see, I've been deep into an investigation. Whew, I shouldn't say anything about this, but of the senator. I think we'll soon have what we need to close the case. I can't tell you any more than that. Just keep your mouth shut for now and wait. Can you do that?"

"I guess." A frown furrowed her forehead. "I ... I don't want him hurt. I really don't."

"Anna, I shouldn't have told you anything, but I don't want you caught in his mess." He paused. "Can you start pulling back from him without him becoming suspicious?"

She nodded. "I, uh, I'll try."

John moved closer to her, gently turned her to face him, and buried his face in her hair. He put his arms around her and held her. She leaned against him, eyes closed, and enjoyed his closeness.

How can I care so much for John when I thought I loved Ken? What do I do?

He pushed her away, smiled, and gently pushed a curl away from her eyes. She looked up at him and forced a smile, but her eyes revealed her pain. He traced a finger down her cheek, following her jaw until his finger reached the tip of her chin. Then he tenderly lifted her head

Chapter 11

Unknown to John and Anna, a navy colored Cadillac parked across the street from her apartment building. Ken sat inside with clenched jaw and angry eyes. He watched as the caterers arrived and when they left the building. A Smith & Wesson .38 Special laid on the seat beside him.

Parked a short distance from the front of the building in an area not lighted by a streetlamp, the dark partially hid his car. The senator slid from the car and crouched behind it to watch John's Explorer. The anger built from the moment he saw John arrive, an overnight bag in hand, and continued to grow. An end to any chance of a romance between Anna and the other man was necessary once and for all. He hid behind a big bush close by and waited.

Sooner than the senator expected, John appeared at the entrance to the apartment building, alone and with his overnight bag in his hand. Ken noticed John was dressed quite differently from when he entered the building. The senator shifted in the bushes to a stance which gave him a better view and waited. When he saw John walking toward the Explorer, Ken took careful aim.

* * *

John placed the bag on the ground as he searched his pockets for his car keys, then picked his bag up, and strode to the Explorer. He put his bag in the Explorer from the passenger side and walked around to the driver's side. As John opened the car door, he heard a gunshot, and a burning pain slammed his shoulder. He threw himself into the SUV, shut the door, and flattened himself on the seat. He put his hand to his shoulder and felt the wet material of his shirt. When John took his hand away, it was covered in blood.

"Shit!" He muttered under his breath.

Reaching for the glove compartment, he opened it, found the Glock he kept there, released the safety, and slowly raised his head barely enough to look up and down the street. All was quiet, and nothing appeared to be moving. No cars suddenly left the vicinity with screeching wheels. No one was running down the sidewalk.

* * *

In the meantime, Ken slipped into the darkness of the building behind him and waited. His heart pounded, but he stifled the panic rising in his throat. "Damn, I don't think I killed him," he mumbled as he hid. "My hand shook too much. Maybe I winged him, though."

* * *

John examined his wound and discovered it was just a graze. "Dammit, someone tried to kill me, but who?" He tore the sleeve off his shirt and pressed it against the wound. "That should stop the bleeding."

He looked around before he started the vehicle and pulled away from the curb. "The would-be killer could be one of two dozen people, but I have a pretty good idea who it was, here outside Anna's place," he muttered. "Yeah, I'm pretty sure who."

He spied the navy Cadillac parked about a block down the street. "What do you know?" He drove past, backed into a driveway, and turned off his headlights. While he waited, he changed his shirt after washing the blood off his arm with bottled water and the rest of his now-torn garment.

* * *

After fifteen minutes, Ken felt safe enough to come out of the darkness. There was no notice taken of the Explorer and that it was gone. The goal was to get away fast and unnoticed. He slipped through the bushes, got in the Cadillac, and drove away. He did not notice the headlights pulling into the road behind him.

Chapter 12

Later, after following the senator a few blocks, John headed for the dark streets of town and waited in the dark. There was an appointment he couldn't miss. When he heard footsteps on the sidewalk, he stepped from the alley. He paused to light a cigarette and squinted at the figure in front of him. With the street light behind him, the man's face was obscured in the darkness.

"Hey, man, didn't know you smoked?" As the man stepped to John's side, the light revealed a bandana tied around his forehead and a hoop earring in his right ear.

"Lots you don't know about me," John replied. "Have you got it?"

"I don't let a good customer down, man."

John held out his hand and waited.

"In a minute, friend, but before we get down to business, got a question for ya."

John's eyes narrowed, and he took another drag on the cigarette. "Business first," he said.

"Hey, man, what's your problem? It's a simple question. You can handle it. Then we can get down to business."

"What is it?" John threw his cigarette on the ground, grinding it out with his shoe.

"The other night, man, you had a chick with you. Good looker, too."

"So?" John was surprised the man knew about Anna's presence that night.

"Your woman?"

"Yeah, why?"

"What's her name?"

John slowly pulled another cigarette from the pack in his pocket and lit it, taking his time. He took a slow draw on it and threw his head back. He glanced down the street, allowing his eyes to linger a few seconds. He turned his attention back to the man.

"Unnecessary information. What's this about?"

"She related to a Tina Kayce?"

"I, uh, don't know. What's this about? Are you talking trouble here?"

"Could be, but never mind. You got the money?" The man pulled a bag out of his pocket and held it up.

John gazed at the man, his brow pulled into a frown, and handed him a bundle of bills wrapped with a rubber band.

The man flipped through the bills, grinned, and handed John the bag.

"Looks right. Nice doing business with ya."

"Hey, what's this about this woman—this Tina something?"

"She's bad news, man. A dead woman." He laughed and disappeared into the darkness, leaving John behind, a deep crease between his eyes.

* * *

After John left her, Anna stared into nothing. *How did I get in such a mess?* She rose from the sofa and paced the floor. *Two men, so different. What's wrong with me? Ken was so good when I needed him.* She paused to brush her fingers over the top of a table. *I … maybe I could have made a better choice, but …* A soft smile played across her lips. *I did love him.*

The smile disappeared. "When did it become past tense? When did the love stop?" She said to the empty room.

Anna poured a fresh glass of wine and curled up on the sofa. She had sipped over half the drink when the doorbell rang. She put her glass on the coffee table next to John's empty one and answered the door.

"Ken!"

"In the flesh," he said and pushed past her.

"What are you doing here?" Her mind raced as her eyes slid past him to the two glasses sitting on the coffee table.

"I wanted to see you. Anything wrong with that?"

"Oh." She answered, voice expressionless. "Of course not."

He turned and stared at her.

"You don't sound glad to see me, Anna. Could it have something to do with the *two* glasses sitting on the coffee table?"

She glared at him. "No, it has more to do with you not being considerate, Ken."

"I see." One side of his mouth twisted into a sneer.

She picked up the two glasses and took them to the kitchen. *Dammit, why do I let him agitate me like this? He doesn't own me. He doesn't.* She sensed him behind her and turned to face him.

"Do you want me out of your life?" His eyes pleaded with her to say what he wanted to hear.

"No," she said. "I don't know." She closed her eyes and sighed. *What do I say? What do I do? His eyes beg …* Anna opened her eyes and tried to smile. *Maybe the man I loved, the man he used to be is still there. Maybe the cruelty …* "I, uh, I don't."

The pained look faded from his face. The senator took a deep breath and exhaled slowly. He reached for her, but his cell phone rang, breaking the moment. After glancing at the name on the screen, he stepped into the living room to answer it. Anna strained to hear what was being said.

"Hello." He kept his voice low. "Okay, I'll be there soon."

When he returned to the kitchen, Anna leaned against the sink, head bowed, staring into the sink as if lost in her own thoughts. She glanced up as he entered the room.

"Everything okay?" she asked.

"Yes, but I've got to go. Something important has come up."

"Now? But it's late. Why would – "

"Don't ask questions, okay? It's business … that's all you need to know."

"Okay." She hoped he didn't notice the relief in her voice.

He slid his arms around her and pulled her against him. He seemed satisfied just holding her, burying his face in her hair for a moment. He kissed her and pushed her gently away. The smile on his face didn't reach his eyes.

"I'll call you tomorrow," he said and left.

Anna waited enough time for Ken to leave the building before she grabbed her purse and rushed to her car. Sliding behind the steering wheel, she turned the key in the ignition. She glanced in the rearview mirror and thought she saw a quick movement behind her car. She turned around and looked but saw nothing, so she pulled out of the parking spot and drove toward the front of the garage without giving it a second thought. She slowed down as she approached the exit. A shadow to her right caught her attention, and she turned her head to see what it was. She heard the passenger door open and automatically put her foot on the brake, slowing the car even more, as the thought hit her, *I forgot to lock the doors.*

Before she could hit the accelerator again, a dark figure jumped in the car so quickly she didn't have time to react. He reached and grabbed the steering wheel while his foot pushed hers away, and he pressed hard on the brake. The car came to a jerking halt.

A hand from behind her covered her mouth with something. A strong, burning smell made her dizzy. She glanced into the rearview mirror. The last thing she saw, before blackness overcame her, were bloodshot eyes staring into hers.

* * *

Anna opened her eyes and quickly closed them. *Ooooh... dizzy.* She opened her eyes again and struggled to focus. *Everything's so blurry.* She carefully turned her head, trying to scan the darkness around her. *Where am I?*

She struggled to sit. A pain much like a sledgehammer striking pierced through her head. "Agggh." She gripped the sides of her head, her eyes clenched tight. As the pain eased, she opened her eyes a slit. She glanced around the darkened room. *This ... this is my apartment.*

A lamp on the opposite side of the room clicked on.

"'Bout time. I thought you was going to sleep all night." A man's voice, gruff and raspy, a smoker's voice, complained.

Anna pulled herself to a sitting position and waited for the dizziness to subside and the queasiness in the pit of her stomach to settle. After a moment she looked at the man, who seemed familiar. She frowned and fought the nausea that crept dangerously close to the top of her throat.

The man, sprawled in one of her chairs, grinned at her, showing brown teeth, one missing in the front. His fingernails, dirty and jagged, tapped the arm of the chair.

"Who are you?" she asked.

"I'm the one asking the questions."

She looked around the room, remembering there were two men in her car. *I've seen him before... in the alley with John.* "Where's the other guy?"

"I'm the only one here." Brown teeth smiled at her.

"What do you want with me?"

"Answers."

"To what?"

"You were with a man the other night, in the alley, by the name of John Mentz. Are you his woman?"

"How did you know I was there?"

"I just know. Now answer my question."

"What was it?"

"Are you his woman?" His voice rose with impatience.

"Of course not." She couldn't tell by his expression if she had successfully masked her surprise at his knowledge of that night. "My car broke down, and he kindly rescued me by taking me home."

"He said you were."

"Well, he can just dream on. I'm not." She paused as a wave of pain swept through her

head. "He did try to get fresh with me, but I managed to ward him off."

"Had you met him before that night?"

"No. Why are you asking these questions?"

He ignored her inquiry. "Yet you had dinner with him tonight."

"Well, yes." His knowing about the dinner surprised her.

"Did he tell you what he does for a living?"

Her body stiffened, and she turned her eyes away from his. He leaned forward in the chair, his gaze intense. She shrunk away from his stare.

"He did, didn't he?"

"No," she said.

"I don't believe you."

Her mind raced. Should she tell the truth or lie? Would he even believe her? But John had been undercover. She couldn't let any one know.

"Okay, okay. He told me he was a lawyer."

A deep, guttural laugh. "What would a lawyer be doing in an alley in that neighborhood?"

"He said he was talking to a client who wouldn't come to his office to answer some questions."

"I see." He stared at her, his brows pulled together in deep thought. After a moment, he walked toward her. She cringed, lowered her head, and wrapped her arms around herself. His fingertips rubbed against her cheek, and he laughed softly. Her body trembled as his fingers continued down her neck and onto her chest. She shrunk further away from him.

He laughed a little louder and removed his hand from her body.

"Whatsa matter? Afraid I might give ya a little?" His voice softened again. "You might even enjoy it, honey. Yeah, purty thing like you. Just might..." His voice trailed off as if lost in his own perverted thoughts.

She whimpered, aware of his closeness, so close she could smell the stench of stale tobacco and body odor. Turning her head away, she closed her eyes against the sight of him and thought of what he might do. *Please, please, just leave me alone. Go away.*

With a sudden chuckle, he stepped away from her as if reading her mind. "You knew what was going down that night."

"I don't know what you're talking about. I only know I was lost and scared out of my wits that night."

"Yeah, sure. Just be certain I won't touch you tonight, babe, but you ever say anything about that night, I'll be back." His raspy voice hardened. "And don't worry, I'll make sure you enjoy it." He walked to the door, but before opening it, he turned back to her, no smile on his face. "Take my advice and forget about that night. Otherwise, you could end up like your sister."

Anna's head snapped up in surprise. She opened her mouth to ask what he meant, but the door closed behind him.

Chapter 13

Earlier that evening Tina turned her car into the garage and stopped, waiting for the gate to open. She looked over her shoulder and saw the black car parked across the street. She had noticed that car before—several times before.

The previous night Tina left her apartment. She didn't clean up the mess her intruders made of the place. Her mind was on finding safety. She settled on a room at a cheap motel on the south side of town rather than take a chance on putting her friends or her sister in danger.

Back home now she drove into her usual parking space, got out of the car, and listened for the beep indicating the doors had locked.

"Hi, beautiful." A big man, tall and wearing dark glasses, had his hat pulled low over his face. Obviously, he tried to disguise his voice.

"Hi." She backed away and tried to go around him.

"You're Tina, aren't you?"

"Who are you?" She continued to try to pass him.

He moved to block her way. "You don't know me."

"I know that. So how do you know me?"

"Your sister."

"You know Anna?" She stopped and looked at him, a quizzical expression on her face.

"Yep. Nice lady."

"How do you know her?"

"I was at her store the other day. She said I should look you up."

"Anna wouldn't do that." Tina's voice rose. An urgent need to escape overwhelmed her, and she tried once again to get around the man.

"Oh, no, you don't," he said. Big hands reached out and grabbed her.

"Let me go!"

"No, honey, I've got important business with you." He covered her mouth with one hand to muffle any screams.

She tried to pry his hands loose, digging her fingernails into his hands and even drawing blood. Unsuccessful, she kicked at him. Her teeth buried into his hand, and he relaxed his grip enough for her to twist around and bring her knee up into his groin. He anticipated her action and quickly moved so her knee hit him in the leg instead. He shoved her, and she fell to the floor. Before she could get back up, he pulled her to her feet. She whirled around, but big, muscular arms wrapped around her. She dug fingernails into them. He grunted in pain, and his grip loosened again, allowing her to slip away. She turned to run.

The strike across the side of her head was the last thing she felt.

* * *

Carl stood over Tina's limp body, rubbing his knee. Her chest was moving so he knew he had not killed her with the blow he gave her to the head.

He furtively looked around but saw no one else in the garage. Tina gave a low moan. A big hand covered her mouth. Satisfied the garage was empty, he got a large piece of plastic from the trunk of his car, placing Tina on it. He pulled out a gun with a silencer, put it to her head, and pulled the trigger. Carl watched her for a moment. Satisfied she was not breathing, he wrapped the plastic around the body and put it in the trunk of his car. A glance over the area did not show any evidence of what had occurred there. He got in the car and drove out of the garage, feeling the body shift as he turned into traffic. After driving a distance from the garage, he pulled out a phone and dialed a number.

"It's done," Carl said.

"Good," Ken said.

"What do you want me to do with the body?"

"Dump it somewhere. I don't care where. Just get rid of it."

"Gotcha. Then what?" Carl said.

"What do you mean? You get out of town, that's what."

There was silence on the other end of the line. A moment passed and Ken said, "Do you understand? Get out of town!"

"Yeah, sure." Carl finally said. "Not sure I'm ready to leave, though."

"You idiot! I said get out of town, and I mean it."

Carl heard the phone click, and he hung up. There was a park ahead, and he turned the car into the entrance of it. A secluded spot was all that was needed now. It did not take long to find one.

* * *

Glad to get that chore over with, Carl headed to Tina's apartment. There was one more thing he wanted to do. He grinned to himself as he thought about how he got the nightie he was going to leave in Tina's apartment. The pleasure he got every time he imagined Anna in that red nightie was almost more than he could take.

He forced his mind back to the chore at hand as he pulled into the parking garage and found an empty space to park. It didn't matter if it belonged to someone who lived there. He wouldn't be long with the task he wanted to do. There was an elevator in the garage so Carl was at his destination in no time. He had managed to get the key from Tina's purse when he was loading her body in his car.

Opening the apartment door, he found a lamp close by to turn on. He looked around at the mess the apartment was in and grinned. This would save him some time. Quickly making his way to the bedroom, he took the red nightie out of his pocket and dropped it on the floor in front of the dresser.

He made his way back to the front door, turning around before opening the door, giving the room one last satisfied glance. Just for good measure Carl turned over a chair and dumped out a couple of potted plants on the floor, kicking the dirt around on the carpet. Satisfied with this, he made sure the lock was turned before shutting the door behind him. But he wasn't through. No, not at all. He wanted more of the woman who really turned him on. Nope, there was no way he could leave without a taste of Anna.

Chapter 14

"Hello." André's voice sounded irritated.

"Andre', it's Anna."

"Oh, hey, Anna. Need a shampoo?"

"Yes, yes, I do—and some conversation."

"Conversation?" He sounded guarded.

"Yes." Anna paused. "Is that all right?"

"Sure. How about four-thirty this afternoon? That's the only spot I have open."

"That'll be fine," she said quickly. "I'll see you then." Anna pushed the end-call button, laid the phone on the desk, and pulled out her accounts payable logbook. In the middle of organizing her thoughts, someone knocked on her office door.

"Come in, Lisa," she called.

"I'm not pretty enough to be Lisa," A deep voice came from the doorway.

Anna glanced up and smiled at the man leaning against the doorframe. The sight of him with a toothpick in his mouth and dressed in a black shirt and black pants left her weak-kneed and wistful.

"But," John said, "I do love just sitting across from you and feasting on your beauty."

Anna laughed and a soft glow spread across her face. "Come in and sit down, John. Is this an official visit or a personal one?"

"Well, I guess personal. I mostly want to sit, stare at you for a while, soak up your charm, and just forget everything else." He pulled a chair next to her, turned it around backward, and straddled it. He propped his chin on his crossed arms as they rested on the back of the chair.

Anna smiled, tilted her head to one side, and shook her head at him.

"I can't think of a better thing to do this morning." He sighed. "Well, I can but I know it's not happening."

"You're terrible!" She laughed, feeling a pleasant warmth go through her.

He threw away the toothpick, stood up, and shoved the chair out of his way. Taking Anna's hand, he pulled her up and into his arms. Silky dark hair slid through his fingers, and his lips brushed her forehead. A slight groan escaped his lips as he pushed his body against hers and her arms slipped around his neck. Her lips glistened as she turned her face upward, eyes closed. His lips found hers, his tongue delving deep into her mouth.

Anna pulled away from him and took a deep breath and slowly exhaled. Her eyes locked with his. Flustered and shaken, in a breathless voice she whispered, "Oh, my."

"Damn, Anna," he asked in a low raspy voice, "can I see you tonight?"

"Yes," she said.

He leaned over, giving her a lingering gentle kiss. "What time?"

"Well, I have a four-thirty hair appointment. How about seven? That should give me time to get home, freshen up, and change clothes."

"Seven it is, then." He grinned, backed away until he reached the door, and put his hand behind him, feeling for the doorknob, his eyes never leaving her. He threw her one last kiss with pursed lips and slipped out the door, closing it behind him.

* * *

The bell above tinkled as Anna opened the door and walked into the salon. Her watch said four twenty-five.

"I hate that bell, Andre'," she called out as she took off her jacket and hung it up.

"You and everyone else. That's why I keep it. Hello, Anna."

"Hello back. You're awful," she replied with a grin.

"And you love it." He laughed. "Sit and make yourself comfortable. It'll be about fifteen more minutes." A petite woman with long blond hair sat in his chair.

Anna picked up a magazine and sat down. Unable to concentrate on the contents of the magazine, she looked around the salon. Glass shelves displayed bottles of various types of shampoo and hair conditioner. Pictures of both men and women with different hair styles stared at her from the walls. Music played softly from some unknown area of the salon. Other than the woman in the chair, she and Andre′ were the only people in the place. Anna half listened to their conversation, but mostly let her mind wander over the last few months. She thought about her feelings for John, about Tina, and about her life in general. She met John three months ago, but she had no doubt she was hopelessly in love with him. Was there the possibility of a future with him, or was that just a dream that would never come true.

"Anna!"

She jumped at the sound of André's booming voice. "Wha...oh, it's you."

"That must have been some daydream, girlfriend." He waved his hand toward the shampoo bowl. "Come, I want to get outta this place. There's a hottie just waiting for my charms to embrace him." Andre′ generally did not flaunt being a homosexual, but he felt comfortable with Anna and often exaggerated the trait when around her.

"I'm sorry. I didn't mean to hold you up." Anna sat in the chair at the shampoo bowl. Neither talked while he shampooed her hair, but afterward, as Andre′ worked, she watched his face in the mirror.

"Are my eyebrows on crooked?" he asked softly.

"No." She laughed. "I didn't mean to be staring. I've had a lot on my mind lately."

"I understand. You've had a lot going on. Decisions can be hard to make sometimes."

Anna lowered her eyes and a warm flush covered her face. *Jeez, does the whole world know about John? How confused I am!*

As if reading her mind, Andre′ said, "Go with your heart, Anna, and get away from the senator. He's trouble."

"You said something to that effect before. What do you know about the senator to make you feel he's, uh, untrustworthy?"

"I know he's running a big drug ring that's getting even bigger and more dangerous." He pressed his lips into a tight line and shook his head. "I shouldn't be telling you this. It's too dangerous."

"Did Tina find this out? Do you know if she's all right?" Anna leaned forward, her eyes looking intensely at his image in the mirror in front of her. "I was told she's dead. Do you know if she is or not? Please, tell me."

He gently placed his hands on her shoulders and pulled her back in the chair. He met her gaze and opened his mouth. At that moment the bell over the door tinkled. Anna and Andre′ turned at the same time to see who had entered. She had a quick glance of a figure dressed in dark clothes and a knit hat covering his face.

She heard Andre′ gasp, then he swung his body around so he was between her and the person at the door. He leaned over her, using his body as a shield, so close she could smell his terror and feel his body shaking. His eyes widened and filled with fear as he stared wordlessly down at her. The explosion of gun shots echoed through the room, and the heavy weight of André's body dropped on her.

"No-o-o-o!" She screamed and shoved him off her, closing her eyes to erase the horror. The doorbell tinkled again as the door closed. André's body fell to the floor with an eerie thud. Anna opened her eyes and stared feverishly around at an empty room. Blood covered her blouse and hands, and she became acutely aware of the silence surrounding her.

* * *

John studied the salon as he walked around it. The body lay beside the chair. The forensics team busily hunted and gathered evidence. Anna in blood drenched clothes sat on the settee situated at the entrance. Her head bowed causing her half-wet hair to fall forward covering her face, shoulders slumped forward. John sat beside her and waited for her to react. She didn't.

"Are you okay?" he asked.

"No, I'm not okay. A friend of mine was just killed. It was horrible. How can I be okay?" She snapped, glancing at him through wet hair from the corners of her eyes. "I never thought you'd ask something so inane." Anna lifted her head to stare at the man beside her. "I thought you'd understand."

"I'm sorry, Anna." John covered her hands, which were clasped in her lap with his hand. "I'm really sorry." He paused before he added, "I hate to ask you now, but we have to know. Do you have any idea who did this? Did you see anything that would help us?"

Anna stared at his hand covering hers. "No, I didn't get a chance to see who it was. Andre′ had me turned slightly away from the door. H-he..." She swallowed, turning her head. After a moment, she turned back to him and continued her story. "He must have seen whoever it was because he suddenly threw himself over me, and I heard shots. I felt the weight of his body. By the time I pushed him off ..." She swallowed again. "Th-the killer was gone."

"You're doing fine. Take a deep breath." John's fingers stroked the back of one of her hands. "Okay, give me your impressions then. Sometimes we think we don't see things, but we have impressions, or we see things we don't remember seeing until you get to talking about what happened. These impressions come from things we see, hear, or even smell that we're not conscious of at the time." John glanced over at the homicide detective who stood close by, taking notes of Anna and John's conversation. The detective looked up at John and nodded.

John turned his attention back to Anna and said, "Now, please, give me your impressions."

"I think I had a quick glimpse of the man just before Andre′ threw himself over me." Her eyes narrowed and brows drew together as she tried to remember. "He was dressed in dark clothes. Yes, yes, they were black, and he had no face." Her triumphant look turned to puzzlement.

"No face? What does that mean, Anna?"

"I, uh, think he had it covered with something. Maybe something like a ski mask."

"All right, what else?"

"I don't know." She shook her head while exasperation edged her voice.

"Did you smell anything? Hear anything?"

"I don't... no, wait. I remember the bell. I heard it just before Andre′ covered me with his body and then again after the shots. I turned to look, but the shampoo bowl blocked my view, though I could see over it a little. I really couldn't see much." She paused and appeared lost in her thoughts. After a few moments she said, "The only smells I remember are just the ones always in the salon." Sighing, she leaned back. "It's hopeless. Nothing I remember is helping."

"It's okay, Anna, You can only do what you can do." He squeezed her hand before he stood and motioned for the homicide detective to join him to one side. They talked in low tones where she couldn't hear them.

But Anna wasn't paying them any attention. Her mind played the whole scene over and over. The color drained from her face, and she sat straight up in the chair.

"John!" Her voice sounded shrill with excitement.

He and the detective rushed over to her, John's face etched with worry and fatigue.

"When I got here, Andre′ seemed irritable and anxious to leave. He ... he said he had someone he was supposed to see tonight and wanted to hurry. He wasn't his usual talkative self. He was rather quiet for a while, but then he started talking. He told me to get away from the senator, that he was trouble. When I asked him about it, he said the senator was running a drug ring, and it was a big one." Anna reached up and grabbed John's arm. He sat down beside her and put his arm reassuringly around her shoulders. She gave a muffled sob as he pulled her closer to him. Then she pulled away from him and said, "Then he told me he shouldn't be telling me all that because it was too dangerous."

John pursed his lips and looked at the homicide detective. "Now we have the motive."

"That was good work, John. She can come in and sign her statement later." The detective walked away, leaving them alone.

"Thanks, Anna. I know that was hard to do, but you gave us some good information. I'll get a policeman to take you home. Will you be all right?" He studied her face and eyes.

"Sure." She tried to smile. "I've made it this far, haven't I? I'll make it the rest of the way. I have to, but right now I just want to go home." Anna heaved a deep sigh. "I ... I just want to go home."

"Hang on, Anna. I need you to keep cool, calm, and collected until I can get this case completed. You're an important factor in this case, so keep yourself together. Soon this will all be over with. I promise."

She gave a small hiccup and wiped her tear-streaked cheeks and mascara-blackened eyes.

"And another thing, it would be a good idea to get the locks on your apartment and on the doors of your shop changed."

"Okay," she said weakly.

"Do you have a security system?"

"Just at the store."

"You might want to get one for your home," he said, "just to be on the safe side."

She bit her lower lip and nodded, quickly looking down at the floor. John gave her a quick hug and went to get her a ride home. Her eyes filled with tears as she watched him walk away.

Chapter 15

Anna changed her clothes and poured a glass of wine. The day had been long and trying; her nerves had taken more than enough. When the doorbell rang, the first glass was gone, and she held the bottle over the glass, filling it again. The sudden sound of the doorbell startled her and some of the wine splattered on the counter. On the second ring, she decided she might as well answer it.

She jerked the door open to find John standing there. He smiled as his eyes took in the sight before him, and she became acutely aware of the revealing nightgown that draped her body. His grin just kept spreading.

"I thought I'd check on you after your experience at the salon." His eyes were looking much too happy so she pulled her robe closer around her.

"Thanks, I appreciate it."

"But you look just fine. Yep, just fine indeed." He stepped inside the doorway and closed the door behind him.

"I am fine. What do you want?" This came out a little sharper than she meant.

His expression turned serious, his lips compressed into a thin line. A stray dark curl fell across his forehead as he sat on the sofa.

"If you don't mind, I could use a glass of that wine you're drinking," he said.

"Sure," she said, "but aren't you on duty?" Anna turned away and went to the bar. Without waiting for an answer from him, she poured another glass of wine and handed it to him.

"Thanks." He took the glass and took a sip. "And no, I'm not on duty tonight."

She threw him a questioning look.

"I asked off so I could be with you. I didn't feel you needed to be alone tonight."

"Oh, John, that is so sweet of you, and I do appreciate it. You're probably right." Her demeanor softened.

Nodding at the glass in his hand, he asked, "How many?"

Anna laughed. "Not that many. This is my second glass, but thanks for caring."

"You're welcome. Now may I make a suggestion?"

"What?"

"Let's take our wine out on the balcony and relax while we look at the moon and the stars. Whadda ya say?" He stood up and took the glass she held before she could reply.

Anna followed him and sat down in one of the lounge chairs, stretching her body out with a sigh. John set the two glasses on the table that was situated between the two chairs and slid into the other chair.

"That is very silly," she said.

"What?"

She took a sip of wine and giggled like a little girl. "Looking at the moon and stars, that's what."

"Hey, there's nothing silly about that. Look at the beauty up there. All those stars look like little diamonds.

"Okay, okay. I give in, especially since you put it that way." She laughed and turned toward him.

Their eyes met for a moment. Her eyes softened, and she reached out. Long, well-manicured fingers grasped his arm.

"I'm so glad you came. You were right. I didn't need to be by myself." She finished her glass of wine and handed her glass to him.

John took it as well as his own glass and refilled both. "I sure hope I know what I'm doing," he mumbled to himself.

"Did you say something?" Anna called out.

He stepped onto the balcony, handed her glass to her, and lowered himself into his chair.

"They are beautiful, aren't they?" Anna gazed at the sky. Her robe had slid open, revealing cream-colored skin and full breasts covered by a lacy nightgown.

"Yes, almost as beautiful as you are," John said softly.

She smiled, her eyes still on the stars above them.

They sat staring at the stars, drinking their wine, and not saying anything. The silence between them was comfortable. Anna felt more relaxed than she had in a long time. All that had happened was pushed out of her mind in this small space of time.

After a while, Anna glanced at John. He appeared to be relaxed and yet there was a guarded air about him. His eyes darted around, and she had the feeling he was listening to every sound. She sighed and turned her eyes back to the sky.

"John?" Anna said.

"Yeah."

"Thanks for being here tonight."

"Sure. No problem."

The silence between them lengthened.

"So," John said, "you want to talk?"

"About what?" Anna got up and leaned against the balcony railing, the lights of the city below sparkling through the wine she held in her hand.

"You know the story of how I met Ken and why I accepted his proposition." She brought her glass to her lips but did not drink the wine that touched against her lips. Instead she turned around to face John.

"I know. That's not what I mean," John said. He got up from his chair and went to her, took her glass from her, and set both glasses on the table.

Anna looked at him with a puzzled frown on her face. She didn't say a word but kept her eyes on his face, not saying a word. Her expression softened as he drew closer to her.

"I want to ask you something," he said. He put his hands on her arms, holding her gently in his hands.

She remained silent, her eyes searching his face for answers, and waited for him to ask his question.

"Do you think you could love a man like me?" He asked, his voice barely audible.

"What did you say?" She wasn't sure she heard what she thought he said.

He cleared his throat. "Do you think you could love a man like me?" He raised his voice.

She smiled and took his hand in hers. "Why would you ever doubt that I could? Of course I could be interested in you." The warm flush of a blush crept up her neck. "In fact, I..."

"You what?"

Anna shook her head, unable to actually say the words. John put a finger beneath her chin and tilted her face upward. His lips brushed against hers as he pulled her tightly against him. Her heartbeat quickened, and her body responded with a passion that matched his.

"Can you say it now?" He said.

Anna pushed him away. She sucked in a deep breath and shook her head at him.

"No, no, I can't," she said. "I'm sorry, John, but I'm not ready. I've got to get some things in my life straightened out first."

"Like Ken. I know, and you're right. I just would like to know if I have any hope." He pulled her close again. "Any at all?"

"Yes, you do." She laughed, meeting his gaze.

"Okay, I can wait, but if I wait, I want you to love me, not just be interested in me."

"I don't think that will be a problem." She slid her hands up his chest and around his neck. Soft lips placed a trail of kisses up his neck to the edge of his lips. They stopped there.

He lowered his eyes until they met hers, and his arms tightened around her. She could feel his desire, and it fueled her passion. Their lips met with the hunger that only love can provide. When they pulled away from each other, Anna took a deep breath in and slowly exhaled, eyes still closed. John tenderly touched her cheek.

"Are you all right?" He said.

"I'm better than all right."

He held her for a moment before they walked into the apartment, arms wrapped around each other. They sat on the sofa. Anna's head rested on John's chest, their hands intertwined. Words between them were not needed for they sensed each other's desires. There was the distant sound of cars riding the streets and a faint aroma of someone cooking dinner. For the first time in quite a while Anna felt her life was normal instead of in turmoil.

* * *

It wasn't long before John realized Anna had fallen asleep. He managed to slip out from under her and eased her onto the sofa. A pillow on the nearby chair was stuffed under her head, and he covered her with an afghan.

John stood over Anna and watched her for a moment. He went to the front door and made sure it was secured. Each room was checked, and then he wandered onto the balcony.

Leaning against the rail, he surveyed the area below. Satisfied that nothing out of the ordinary was out and about, he went to the kitchen and got a beer out of the refrigerator.

The most comfortable chair was across from the sofa where Anna lay. Her sleep was a restless one. The moans that came from her worried John as he knew what nightmares were like. They came, but they didn't easily go. She had not really grieved, and it was what she needed to do. When it hit her, he wanted to be there. He wanted to be the comfort she would need and the outlet for her anger.

He stood up and went for another beer. He drank and watched over her, aching to hold her, and he drank some more. Soon he dozed off.

A loud crash woke him. He shook his head trying to clear his mind and looked through bleary eyes at the light coming from the kitchen. Another loud crash brought him to his feet, and he ran to the kitchen to find Anna sitting in the middle of the kitchen floor, pots and pans scattered all around her. She looked up at him, eyes red and swollen, her face wet. She picked up a pot close to her and threw it against the wall. Her hands covered her face and the sobs that came from her were loud and hard.

John cleared a pathway through the debris. He knew it would come and hoped that it wouldn't hit her so hard, but he knew it would. It was bound to. She had controlled it far too long. He sat in the floor beside her and gathered her into his arms, rocking back and forth as if she were a child.

"Hey, baby, it's okay. You just cry it all out of your system. Come on, let it all out. You'll feel better for it."

From a trembling body came a sob, and as he rocked with her, she gradually calmed down.

"John, how did I manage to get my life in such a mess? Poor Andre'. He died trying to warn me. Everything my sister tried to tell me was true. It shouldn't have taken the death of a good friend to make me see what was right before my eyes." Anna held onto him tightly.

"I know, sweetheart, but you didn't have control over the things that happened. You believed in your loyalty to Ken."

"That damn asshole!" She swung her fist against John's chest and did not hear the grunt of pain he gave. "I'll kill him. I swear I'll kill him."

"Hey, don't talk like that. You don't mean it." John pushed her away from him and looked her in the eyes. "Do you hear me? DO...NOT...TALK...LIKE...THAT!" He shook her gently until she nodded that she heard him. He pulled her to him and held her until he felt her body become limp against him.

"Come on," he said, "let's put you to bed where you can rest better." He helped her up and led her unsteady body to the bedroom. Gently he helped her into the bed.

John rummaged through the bathroom cabinet until he found something to help her sleep. With a glass of water in one hand and pills in the other, he went to the bedroom, got her to take one of the pills, and tucked her into her bed. He pulled a chair close and sat there until she was sleeping soundly. Pulling a pillow down on the floor beside the bed, he laid down and closed his eyes.

Sometime later, he quietly got up and went through her apartment checking the doors and listening for any unusual sounds. The kitchen floor was still a mess, so he picked up all the pots and pans and put them back in the cabinet. He flipped the light off and walked back to the bedroom in the dark.

Anna's chest rose and fell in the slow rhythm of sleep. He resisted the urge to lie beside her.

"I love you, Anna," he muttered to the sleeping figure in the bed. "Damn, what a mess."

He laid down on the floor, folded the pillow in half, stuffed it under his head, and closed his eyes, but sleep wouldn't come. Periodically he would make his rounds through the apartment and onto the balcony for a smoke. Mostly, though, his mind went through the details of the case. They needed more evidence. He was determined to make his case stick and put the senator behind bars for good. And then maybe, just maybe, Anna would see she loved him, not the senator.

"I think she's beginning to see the senator for what he really is. She'll become more enlightened and soon," he muttered under his breath.

Chapter 16

Anna stood in front of the police department. The sun bore down warmly on her, and she was feeling a little uncomfortable in the red linen suit she wore. It was ten steps to the door, and each one brought back a memory of the afternoon before. When Anna reached the top, she stopped and took several deep breaths before opening the door.

The cool air that hit her when she entered felt good. Tightening her lips in determination, she pulled together the courage to walk to the desk and explain her mission. She was escorted to an office and told to have a seat and wait for the detective. She didn't wait very long.

The detective was very young. He shuffled papers around and finally settled on one paper in particular which he handed to her with a pen.

"Read this statement carefully, Ms. Kayce. Don't sign it if you think of something to add to it or if you don't agree with what the statement says." The detective laid the typewritten sheet in front of her with a pen. "If everything sounds accurate and complete, sign where I've checked."

Anna nodded and picked up the paper and read it. After a moment she laid the paper down. She sat, pen poised over the statement, and bit her bottom lip.

"Is there a problem?" The detective watched her closely.

"No, I'm just thinking. I want to make sure I give you all the information."

"That's good. Is there anything I can do to help?"

"No, I don't think so." She signed the statement and sat back, sighing her relief.

"Thanks for coming in." The detective picked up the paper and tucked it in a folder. "Be careful, Ms. Kayce."

"Oh, I will. I certainly will." Her voice broke, and she turned her head away.

Anna left the police department. Signing her statement was not a hard chore, instead it was a relief to get it done. However, Tina was still weighing on her mind. She was feeling a great weight on her shoulders and a certain amount of guilt. The death of Andre' and maybe even her sister could have been avoided if she had just listened and believed. Promising herself a long vacation when all this was over, she got in her car.

Traffic was heavy and gave her time to think. Her mind wandered back to the night before. John gave her so much support. The outburst she had in the kitchen was embarrassing to remember. John didn't appear surprised by it. On the contrary, he seemed to expect it.

Anna brought her attention back to the traffic. Satisfied with her progress through it, her mind drifted back to the night before. A warm feeling came over her at the memory of John asking her if she could love a man like him. She ran a quick comparison of Ken and John. Anna smiled at the conclusion she came to and knew within her heart what her decision was, but first she had to find out where Tina was, what may have happened to her. She could not get on with her life until she did. And she would. There was no doubt in her heart about that. Her smile faded at this thought.

Chapter 17

Several days later, John parked his car parallel to the curb and turned off the engine. He sat in the dark. By the lights of oncoming cars, he watched the house across the street, the yard bare of any flowers or bushes. Children's toys littered the front yard of the wood-framed house, and a baby's playpen filled the small porch.

Down the street sat a dark colored car. The lights of a passing car revealed a man slouched behind the wheel, a hat pulled down low over his forehead.

John lit a cigarette and watched the car. A few moments later he saw the glow of a cigarette in one of its windows. The signal. He got out of his car, threw his cigarette on the pavement, and ground it out with his shoe.

The house, dark except for a small rim of light around the edge of a blind, had no doorbell, so John knocked on the door. He heard the scraping of a chair on the floor and then footsteps. The door opened a crack, and a bloodshot eye stared out at him.

"Yeah?" a gruff voice asked.

"I'm buying."

The door closed, and John heard a chain lock being unlatched before the door swung open. A big black man stood in the doorway, a tight green tee shirt covering bulging muscles. A long scar went from his right eye down diagonally to his jaw.

"Got the money?" the man asked.

"Yeah, I got it."

The man stood to the side and motioned for John to enter the house. The small living room contained a well-worn sofa, a television set, a table and lamp, and an old trunk obviously being used as a coffee table. Only blinds covered the window, no curtains. A strong odor of cabbage cooking mixed with another unidentifiable odor assaulted John's nasal passages.

Green Shirt closed the door and turned to face the newcomer. He looked John over from head to toe, then with a grunt he let his body fall onto the sofa. John sat down beside him. On the trunk in front of them, some white powder and a razor blade lay on white paper.

"Take a snort," the man offered John.

"Uh, no thanks, I wanna take it with me."

A big black woman in a hot pink tent dress shuffled into the room. She nodded at John, handed Green Shirt a can of cheap beer, and dropped her ample body in the chair. It gave a loud creak as her full weight settled in the cushions.

Oh, she's got to weigh at least 300 pounds if not more. John stifled a grin and turned his gaze away.

Green Shirt scolded her, "Woman, don't ya know we got a visitor?"

"So? I don't know him," she said.

"Ya suppose to git a beer for him, too. Now git your lazy ass up and go git him one."

"That's okay," John replied, wanting to get the deal completed and leave. "I really don't want one."

"Yeah, man, a cold beer would be good. She'll get it."

The woman got up with a grunt and shuffled from the room, muttering under her breath. After a few moments she returned with another can of beer and handed it to John. Then the chair gave another dying creak as she lowered her massive body into it again.

John took a sip of the cool beer, then turned to Green Shirt and said, "Can we get back to business now? I got another appointment."

"Yeah, man, wadda ya want? Reefer? Coke? Maybe some smack? I got it all and if I don't, I know where ta get it." He grinned. His teeth were a couple of shades lighter than his skin. One tooth was broken in half and turning black.

"About three ounces of crack."

Green Shirt nodded at him, downed the last of his beer, and left the room. When he returned, he shoved the white powder on the trunk aside, set a small bag of cocaine down with all the paraphernalia to inject it in a vein.

John leaned forward and put his hand out to pick up the small bag.

"Money first," Green Shirt said.

"Sure, sure." John took his wallet out, pulled out a wad of money, and handed it to the man.

While Green Shirt counted the money, John opened the bag and dipped his finger in the powdery contents. "Looks like good stuff."

"The best money can buy." Green Shirt grinned at him and put the money in his pocket. He nodded toward the bag. "Try it."

"I'd rather wait till I get home."

Dark brown eyes narrowed in guarded suspicion, and Green Shirt leaned toward him. "I said try it."

"Okay, no problem." John reached for the paraphernalia and the bag. "Hey, man, I don't like shootin' up in front of people. It's a private thing with me. Where's the bathroom?"

Green Shirt pointed down a dark hallway, and John followed his direction. Midway down the hallway he found a door which opened into a tiny dingy bathroom. From his jacket pocket he drew out two small packets. The first one he opened contained salt, which he poured into his hand. Leaning over the sink, he rubbed his eyes with the salt until his eyes were sufficiently red. Next he opened the other packet and sniffed pepper deep into his nose, causing him to sneeze and his sinuses to drain. Staggering his way back to the living room and wiping his nose on the back of his sleeve, he reclaimed his seat on the sofa next to the huge black woman, who had moved to the sofa in his absence. He leaned back allowing his head to roll toward her.

"Yup, that's mighty good stuff." He grinned at Green Shirt, who grinned back at him.

"It comes from a good source. You can't beat it." The black man raised his beer can in a salute.

"Where you get your stuff?" John laughed, his head rolling against the back of the sofa. "Love that good stuff." His voice faded, and he seemed unaware of the man and woman sitting close by. He heard a deep guttural laugh next to him.

"Hell, he'd be surprised to know where it came from." The woman's voice sneered.

"Shuddup, woman," Green Shirt said.

"Huh? Did you say something?" John rolled his head back toward the woman, focused red eyes on her, and grinned. "Makes a little woman look mighty purty. Yeah, mighty good stuff." Then he leaned toward her, placing his hand on her ample knee, and slid his hand up her leg.

She slapped his hand and tried to scramble up off the sofa.

"Hey," Green Shirt said, "git yo grimy hand off my wife." He heaved his big body up, grabbed John by the shirt, and pulled him up onto his feet. "Out you go, you bastard, and don't come back." John managed to grab his bag of cocaine before Green Shirt threw him out the door.

* * *

John slid behind the wheel of his Chevy Cavalier. He lit a cigarette and glanced down the street. The glow of a cigarette was evident, and John inserted the key in the ignition and started the car. He slowly pulled away from the curb. He took a circuitous route to his destination, keeping a close eye on the traffic in all directions. When he felt confident he was not being followed, he drove into the parking lot of a busy shopping strip. At the far end of the strip, red neon lights outlined the painted windows of a nightclub. Blue neon lights centered in the window announced the name of the nightclub, as a steady line of people entered and exited Richie's Bar and Grill.

He entered the club and ordered a beer. He sat at the bar, and when a sufficient amount of time passed, he finished his beer and left the bar. The cool night air felt good after the stuffiness of the smoke-filled room he just left. He breathed in the fresh air, stretched his arms, and nonchalantly looked around the parking lot. He walked to his car, stopped, and lit a cigarette before opening the door. The car window of the car next to him rolled down.

"I think we've got him with this one. Check out the encircled crown on the bag." John reached in his pocket and handed the bag of cocaine to the dark figure in the car. "And check for prints. You know, just in case."

The window rolled up, and the car pulled away as John unlocked his car door and slid behind the wheel.

* * *

The next morning Anna arrived at the store late. Lisa had already opened and was helping a customer when Anna walked by her.

"Good morning, Lisa. Sorry I'm so late."

"Oh, hey, listen, Anna, there's someone waiting to see you."

Anna turned around with a look of surprise on her face. "Who is it?"

"I think it's a policeman. Anyway, I put him in your office with a cup of coffee and a donut."

"You wonderful woman. You brought donuts."

"Yup, I did. Your favorite kind, too."

"Chocolate glazed donuts," they said in unison, then laughed.

On her way to her office, Anna stopped by the coffee maker, poured a cup of coffee with sugar, and picked up two donuts, placing them on a paper plate. When she opened the door, John looked up at her, his mouth full, and chocolate glaze smeared on each side of his mouth.

"These donuts must be good." She laughed and set her coffee cup and plate on her desk. Shoving her purse in a bottom drawer, she seated herself in the leather desk chair. "You look as if you have something to tell me. I hope it's something good."

"Uh, hmmm, I think in a way it is."

"You think? That doesn't sound too promising."

John shrugged his shoulders but gave her no assurances.

Anna sighed and took a sip of her coffee. "Okay, guess I have to take it like a woman. Give it to me."

"We have the proof we need on the senator for drug trafficking and distributing." John watched her closely.

A shade shuttered her expression, and she lowered her eyes. "I see," she said softly.

"But..." He waited, still watching her.

She quickly glanced up at him, waiting for him to finish his sentence. The room felt stuffy and perspiration gathered on her upper lip.

"But we're not going to prosecute him for it right now."

"Why not? I mean what's the point in waiting?"

"I can't discuss the case with you at this point, but we're holding off until we complete our investigation on a few things, like your sister's disappearance."

"Oh, okay. I-I understand."

"Are you okay with that?"

"Yeah, I guess so." She gave him a small smile. "I don't really have a choice about it, do I?"

"Just please, Anna, be careful, keep your mouth shut, and let us handle this. Okay?" He shoved his hands in his pockets as he rose from his seat.

Her hardened eyes met his. "I will, but make damn sure you get him."

"I fully intend to do just that."

* * *

After John left her, Anna sat in deep thought. *Could it be almost over,* she thought. *And then what?*

But it wasn't over yet. And she wasn't a person to just sit and wait. Not anymore. Anna grabbed her jacket and purse, locked her desk, and waved at Lisa on her way out of the store.

Lisa looked after her in surprise. "Do you want me to close or will you be back?" She asked in a loud voice.

"Yes, please, close up for me. I don't know when I'll be back."

"Okay. No problem."

"I promise I'll make it up to you." Anna yelled as she pushed open the door.

"Oh, don't worry about it." Lisa said, but Anna was gone.

Chapter 18

The hallway was quiet as Anna slipped her key into the door of her sister's apartment. The door swung open to an uneasy darkness.

"Oh, God, something's not right. Tina hates darkness. She would never leave her curtains closed like this," Anna stepped into the apartment, a bad feeling in the pit of her stomach. "If I had come over ..." She shivered. "I would have known sooner is all." A wave of guilt swept through her.

"Hello," she called out from just inside the doorway. When there was no answer, she nervously stepped further into the living room. In the dimness, she could see the disarray. Turning on a lamp close to her, she looked around the room and gasped.

Something or someone had tossed a chair on its side, toppled the magazine rack beside it upside down, and had strewn magazines across the floor. Several turned-over potted plants left dirt spread across the floor. The room had been ransacked with a lamp lying on its side and pictures on the wall askew.

Her heart pounded in fear. *What? What's happened?* With shaking hands, she opened the bedroom door. The darkness smothered her, but she forced herself to step into the room and flip on the light. With a gulp, she swallowed the lump caught in her throat and looked around. The dusty rose silk comforter lay on the floor at the end of the bed, and the white lace sheets were strewn across the mattress. The dresser drawers hung open, their contents spread on the floor. Anna stooped down and picked up a red silk gown from the floor. Its bodice was covered with lace roses. She gasped, dropped the gown, and stood up quickly. It lay in a heap at her feet. Anna swallowed back the panic and forced herself to stay calm. Her head throbbed in pain, but she compelled her mind to focus. She stepped over the gown and continued her search. A music box lay on its side, and a few notes of music tinkled when Anna set it upright on the dresser. The vanilla scent of a candle still lingered in the air.

"Tina?" She eased over to the bathroom and opened the door. "Tina?"

Going back to the living room after finding no sign of her sister, she sat on the edge of the sofa. On the coffee table in front of her lay a magazine. She noticed the edge of a piece of paper sticking out between the pages. Anna picked up the magazine and thumbed through it, looking for the page the paper was marking. The piece of paper fell to the floor. Alarm swept over her, and her muscles turned into tight knots as she picked it up and looked at the familiar handwriting.

I told you to shut up about it and I meant it. You've gone too far. Now you'll die.

There was no signature, but Anna knew who had written it. The handwriting was as familiar to her as her own. She slipped the note in her pocket and took a few deep breaths to compose herself. Hands shaking, she dialed Tina's cell phone. It rang numerous times with no answer. She hung up and dialed 911, still fighting the panic overtaking the calm exterior she tried to maintain.

* * *

The police didn't take long to get there. They searched the apartment finding no signs of Tina or where she could be.

"Could she have torn her apartment up like this herself?" one policeman asked.

"No! No way. Tina was a neat freak." Anna retorted, angry at his attitude.

She looked up and saw John standing behind the policeman. Her control began to crumble, and the tears streamed down her pale, drawn face. John said something in a low voice, and the policeman nodded as he turned and left the room. John walked over and stood by her.

"Oh, God, I'm so glad you're here. H-how did you know to come here?"

"I have my informants," he said as he took her by the arm and pushed her down on the sofa. He sat down beside her. The look on his face stopped her from saying anything more. John tenderly touched her lip with his finger. She pulled away from him and turned her head to the side. "Who hurt you, Anna? Why didn't you tell me about it when I was at your store? Why didn't I see this then?"

"It's nothing. And anyway makeup does wonders."

"Tell me who did it." He cupped her face in his hand and pulled her head back toward him. She had no choice but to look him in the eyes.

"Ken hit me in anger. He wouldn't have done it if he hadn't been so angry."

"Was he angry because of me?"

"Yes." Her voice was barely audible.

"I ought to kill the bastard."

"Don't talk like that. Please." She turned frightened eyes on his face. "It, well, it helped me see what he really is."

John rubbed one hand over his chin. "Anna, I have to tell you something."

"What?" She stared at him. His expression left her cold.

"Anna..."

"Oh, God! What's wrong?" She choked back her fear.

"I'm sorry." He pulled her to him and wrapped his arms around her. "Your sister is dead."

Her body shook uncontrollably as she cried. Eventually she turned tear-filled eyes to him. The expression on her face asked the question in her mind. How?

"Her body was found in Ledfield Park by some hookers. She had a blow to the head and had been shot."

"Do you know why?" Her voice cracked with the effort to control her emotions.

"No, Anna. We were hoping you could give us a clue or a lead."

"I don't..." She stopped, her eyes widened.

"What is it?"

She shook her head.

"Anna, if you know anything at all, please tell me. If you don't feel comfortable telling me, I can get someone else to talk to you."

"No, it's not that, John."

"Then what?"

"I have to explain something to you first." She pulled away from him.

"I'm listening."

She pulled her body up straight and wiped her eyes and nose. Averting her eyes from his, she began.

"Some years ago, I lost my job, just about lost everything. I told you about that. I had been kicked out of my apartment, my car had been repossessed, unemployment had run out. And the list goes on. Anyway, I was pretty much destitute. I met Ken, I mean Senator Levall, at a party I'd gone to. We were introduced by a mutual friend and hit it off. I guess it was the booze, I don't know, maybe he just made me feel comfortable talking to him, but I told him all about myself and the predicament I was in with my business and my finances. He called me a few days later with a proposition."

John sat silent, looking at her with searching eyes.

"He—he gave me a car, an apartment, some money in a bank account, and a credit card. Eventually he set me back up in a successful business."

"What was the price you had to pay for all these favors?"

"I—I became his mistress."

"I see." His voice was low. "Thought so, and heard rumors, but hearing it..."

"By the time that happened, I was in love with him, or at least thought I was."

Silence.

"But then things started changing." She looked at him, eyes pleading for him to understand. "He became not so gentle anymore, and he kept sending me on these ... these deliveries."

"Deliveries?"

"Yes."

"What did you deliver?"

"It was just a real thick envelope. Felt as if it had money or something like that in it." She covered her eyes. "I was so stupid, just so stupid."

John reached over and took Anna's hands in his. "Anna, this is important. Did you ever receive anything in return for that envelope?"

"Just a message to take back to Ken. He always insisted I have a message to give to him. I figured this was to prove I actually delivered the envelope. It was all so silly to me."

"What was this message?"

"Well, it's kind of hard to say," Anna said.

"What do you mean?" John waited patiently as he watched Anna struggle to keep back the tears of grief and focus on what he was asking of her.

"It was just a number or sometimes a symbol and a couple of words."

"Symbol?"

"Yes, like a triangle or a square. It was always different, never the same. The numbers were single digits, even though once I had one that was a double digit. Like I said, it was all so silly, so childish." Anna covered her mouth with her hand and her eyes grew wide.

"What is it, Anna?" John gently pulled her hand away from her mouth.

"I can't believe I forgot about it."

John waited for her to go on, not really expecting it to be anything of significance.

"The tape Tina gave me. I never looked at it."

"Where is this tape?" He couldn't hide his excitement over this bit of information.

"It's at my office locked up in my desk drawer."

"I need that tape, Anna."

She got her purse and pulled out a ring of keys. "These are to the store. This little one will open my desk. The tape is in the bottom right drawer." She handed him the keys and sat down again.

"The message was just a plain piece of paper, nothing special or out of the ordinary. You know what I mean, it had no printing or heading on it. Just a plain piece of paper."

"Did it have any writing on it at all?"

"Well, no, it looked more like the symbol or number had been stamped on the paper. The night you rescued me I was making a delivery."

"Okay. Is that all you need to tell me?"

"No." She took a deep breath before continuing. "You know what happened with the last delivery." She blew out a breath. "Then…"

He nodded and waited for her to go on.

"There was a man – no, two men – who forced their way into my car, covered my face with something strong-smelling that knocked me out."

"Sounds like ether. When did this happen?" Ken asked.

"The night of our dinner." She touched her lip. "The same night Ken did this." She tried to smile, but grimaced instead. "I, uh, I decided to go see Tina."

"Okay, go on." No answering smile crossed his face.

"I woke up back in my apartment. There was only one man with me, and he questioned me about you and what went on the night I met you. I told him about you rescuing me."

"What did he want to know about me?" John appeared tense, even eager, leaning slightly toward her.

"Just if I had known you before that night."

"What else?"

"He also told me that you said I was your woman."

"Yes, I did, sorry. I thought that would satisfy him, and he wouldn't ask any more about your presence there."

"Well, I denied it."

"I see." He frowned and looked thoughtful. "What did he say then?"

"He wanted to know if I knew what you did for a living." She shrugged. "Since I didn't think you wanted him to know the truth, I told him you were a lawyer and was there that night to talk to a client who wouldn't come to your office."

"Good thinking."

"Yes, I don't know if he believed me or not, but he let it go at that."

"Okay."

Anna wrapped her arms around herself. "There's something else."

"What is it?"

"I found a red nightgown on the floor of Tina's bedroom."

"So?" he asked impatiently.

"I sold that nightgown to a man the other day. He may have been the person who killed Tina."

"My God, Anna, that means he knows who you are."

"I know." Her voice cracked as she spoke, eyes wide with fear.

"Wait a minute! You said you sold a nightgown to him. Did he pay by credit card?"

"No, he paid cash."

"Oh." Disappointment.

"Did you write his name on the receipt, by any chance?" He said.

"No. I just wanted to get rid of him as quickly as possible. He was creeping me out."

"Damn. Can you describe him?"

"He was a big man, over six feet tall, blond, blue eyes. I'm not good at guessing someone's weight. Oh, he said his name was Carl. He didn't give a last name."

"Okay, do you think you would be able to recognize him if you saw him again?"

"I think so. Wait! I remember Tina saying something about a new love in her life. I didn't get to meet him, but she described him. He was tall, blond, and had blue eyes."

"Think it was the same man?"

"I don't know." Anna shook her head and frowned. "She never told me his name."

"Okay. Go on with your story."

The man in my apartment, he..." She paused and closed her eyes tightly.

"What, Anna?" He prompted.

"Well, he … he threatened me."

"How?" His voice broke on the one word.

Anna opened her eyes to glance at him. There was a slight twitch in his jaw as he gritted his teeth. "He, uh, told me he knew that I was aware of what was going on that night. He told me not to ever say anything or he would—anyway, he told me I could end up like my sister. I didn't know what he was talking about."

"Was your sister into drugs?"

"No, no way."

"What made Tina suspicious of the senator?"

"I don't know." Anna fought tears. "I only know she had been suspicious of Ken for a long time. She thought he was into something illegal, but I don't think she had any idea for sure what it was. I don't think she did." Anna gazed at the man beside her. "She would have told me sooner if she did, I'm sure. She'd been begging me not to have anything else to do with him, but she'd never been able to get any solid proof that he was doing anything illegal. I told her until she could give me proof I owed him my loyalty. She vowed she'd get that proof." She shook her head. "It killed her. I killed her. Why didn't I listen?" Her voice faded.

"Anna, we've been investigating this drug ring for quite awhile now. We suspect Senator Levall is connected, and the deliveries you've been making are money drops for the drugs."

"But I never received anything but that so-called message to take back to Ken." Anna covered her eyes with a shaking hand. "I've been so stupid, so dumb. I didn't know. I promise I didn't know."

"I know you didn't. The drugs were delivered elsewhere as soon as you dropped the money off."

"How do you know this?"

"The department has been watching you for quite some time." John reached for her hand and moved it away from her eyes. "Is it possible your sister got involved with this drug ring?"

"You've been watching me? So you already knew about Ken and me?" Anna dropped her eyes to stare at her lap before she answered his question. "No, Tina would never take or deal in drugs." She looked thoughtful for a moment and then shook her head as if answering a question in her mind.

"I told you I'd heard rumors ... but, that's for later." He shrugged. "Tell me." John cupped her jaw in his hand and turned her face toward him. Her eyes met his and widened just noticeably.

"Tell me." His voice was firmed.

"Tina was trying to get in touch with me. Like I told you, she left me messages on my answering machine at home. I don't know why she didn't call me at the shop or call my cell phone, but she didn't. I didn't get her messages until I got home that night. She said it was important, but I never found out what it was. When I did get her, she couldn't talk. I think someone was there with her."

"It's possible she found out about the drug connection, maybe even confronted him with it so he would leave you alone," John said.

"Could be. I don't know, but the last voice mail I got she sounded fine and said the love of her life was keeping her busy and that she would call me and we'd have lunch. She didn't mention anything about what it was that she needed to talk to me. It was kind of strange after the message I had gotten before."

"Okay. That's enough for right now. Go home and get some rest. I'll be by later to check on you."

She stood up, turned to John, and asked, "But why did that man buy a nightgown and leave it in her apartment?" She gasped. "Was she murdered and raped here and then dumped elsewhere?"

"She wasn't raped, Anna, and we don't think she was murdered here, but we won't know for sure until we have a chance to investigate further. He probably bought the nightgown as an excuse to see you. He most likely left it in her apartment to let you know he was the one who killed your sister and you're next."

"Oh, my God!"

"We'll get him, Anna."

She looked at him with eyes filled with fear, turned as if to leave but stopped. Slowly she turned to face him. "You've been following me?"

"Yes. Not necessarily me every time but someone from the precinct. I'm sorry. It had to be done." His eyes begged her to understand.

"I-I guess I understand." With that she walked out the door.

John turned to one of the policemen and said, "Follow her and keep an eye on her. I'll send relief in a little while."

Chapter 19

Anna opened the door to her apartment and stepped through it. The darkness enveloped her with a dispirited and depressing hollowness that made her shiver. Drained and empty, she remained still for a moment, listening to the silence of the room. Then she turned on a lamp and lowered her body onto the sofa with a sigh. She felt exhausted beyond the point of crying. She slipped her shoes off, lay down on the sofa, and curled into a fetal position. The heaviness of grief filled her heart, and the tears began to flow. Her body shook with uncontrollable sobs, and she let her grief cry itself out. Then the soft fingers of sleep danced over her body until the blackness of welcomed oblivion wrapped its arms around her.

And she slept.

Something awakened her abruptly. Confused, she opened her eyes and glanced around. Terror clutched at her, but she wasn't sure why. The doorbell rang again, and, shaking the cobwebs out of her head, she realized that was what had disturbed her sleep. With a moan she got up from the sofa and went to the door.

"Hi." John stood outside the door, a brown envelope in his hand.

"Hi." She tried to smile. "Excuse my appearance."

"Feel better?" he asked. "You needed the rest."

"I suppose, thanks. At least as good as I can. What have you got there?"

"I've some pictures here. Thought maybe you'd look at them and see if you can identify anyone."

"Okay. Come in." She turned and walked back to the sofa.

John shut the door and followed her. Sitting beside her, he leaned down and picked up a piece of paper on the floor.

"Here," he said, "guess you dropped this."

She took it from him and laid it on the coffee table. Pausing for only a split second, she picked it up again and opened it.

John watched her with a puzzled expression on his face.

"Jeez, I must be exhausted. I totally forgot about this," she said and handed the paper to him.

He opened and read it.

"Where did you get this?" He said.

"I found it in Tina's apartment stuck inside a magazine. I put it in my pocket and forgot about it after you told me she was—was—gone."

"I need to see if they can pick up some fingerprints from it. Maybe it will lead us to whoever wrote it. I suspect that person is the one who killed Tina."

"I can tell you who wrote it."

He glanced at her in surprise.

"Are you serious? You recognize the handwriting?" he asked.

"Yes."

"Who?"

"Ken."

John looked at her, his eyes staring deep into hers. Without a word, he handed her the envelope.

"What is this?" She drew back and looked at the envelope as if it were covered with some terrible disease.

"The pictures. Remember, you're to look at them and see if there are any you can identify."

"Oh, yes, I'm sorry. I'm not thinking straight right now. Sure, I'll look at them." Anna took the envelope from him, opened it, and dumped the pictures onto the sofa between them. She spread the photos so she could look at them all at one time. She picked each one up and scrutinized it closely. One, in particular, caught her attention, and she stared at it long and hard.

"Do you recognize that one?"

"Yes. This is the man who was in my apartment after I had been drugged in my car." She handed the picture to him.

"He's a strong arm for the senator, Anna."

"Strong arm?"

"Yes, and we're on to him. Look at the rest of the pictures, Anna. See if you can identify this Carl you were telling me about. He may very well be your sister's murderer."

She picked up the next picture, staring at it before putting it down again and picked up the next. As she neared the last of the pictures, she paused, and with trembling hands, handed one to John.

"John, this is him! The man at my store!"

John took it and stared at the picture as if memorizing it. "Yes, this is Carl Blakely, professional killer," he said.

"Oh, my God!"

"You got it. A hit man. He may very well be the one who killed your sister. We managed to find some DNA. Evidently she fought her attacker. There was skin and blood under the fingernails of her right hand. They're trying to match them now." He gathered up the pictures and put them back in the envelope. "You've been a big help, Anna."

"I'm glad. I want the killer of my sister. I'll do whatever it takes."

"Good. Oh, they were able to determine that Tina was killed in the garage. They found traces of her blood. She was probably getting either into or out of her car, was approached by the killer on some pretence, murdered, and her body taken to the park and dumped. The murderer probably wanted it to look as if she had been murdered in the park."

Anna was silent for a moment before saying, "Okay, thanks for telling me."

"By the way, I got that tape Tina gave you. It verifies the senator's part in the drug ring. With that and the evidence we collected... well, there's no way he can beat it. We've got him, Anna."

"What about my sister?"

John's expression turned solemn. "We're still working on that, but we'll get him. I promise you that. We're being very careful because we want to make sure our case will stick."

"I know," Anna said and frowned. She shook her head. "But why tear up the apartment like that?"

"Well, I think Carl may have been looking for that tape. We're not really sure if Carl was the one who ransacked your sister's apartment. It looks more like there was more than one person. Probably the same guys who hijacked your car and drugged you. You know, the ones in the green sedan. We hope to pick them up soon. Anyway, with the other information we've managed to collect, we have him. Now we've got to find whoever killed Tina and connect him to the senator. I'm sure this Carl was the killer."

"If Ken had my sister killed, you must prove it. He can't go scot free. Promise me, John, that you will get him."

"We're working on it, Anna. If he had her murdered, I'll get him."

"If you don't," she said through clenched teeth, "I will." Her hands balled into fists, and her body trembled with anger.

John put his arms around her. His hand slowly rubbed her back until he felt the tense muscles ease under his touch.

"Don't do anything drastic, please. Just leave it up to me. I'll get him," John said. "I promise, I *will* get the son of a bitch."

* * *

Anna watched John until the door closed behind him. She locked the door, poured a glass of wine, and turned out all the lights. She went out on the balcony and lowered her body onto the soft cushion of a lounge chair. The lights of the city were all the company she had as she drank glass after glass of wine. The affects of the wine began to blot out the memories that her brain could not shut out, and the tears came. *Damn! When am I going to quit crying.* When she cried all the tears she had, anger took their place. She went inside and paced back and forth, her anger building.

"I'll kill the bastard," she said to the empty apartment. She drank the last of the wine in her glass and threw it at the fireplace. "I am so sorry, Tina. If I had just listened to you, you might be alive today. I'm such an idiot!"

Anna curled up on the sofa and imagined all the ways she could kill the man who gave her the life she enjoyed and then destroyed it. The wine took its affect, and she eventually fell asleep, a sleep filled with uneasy dreams.

* * *

John went back to the police department and wrote up his report. When he left there, he drove to the senator's home. He turned off the motor and sat in the dark watching the house.

It was dark, but the light was on in several windows. A shadow appeared in one of them, and John's hand tightened on the steering wheel.

"I'll get you, you son of a bitch," he mumbled under his breath. "Even if I have to kill you myself."

The shadow moved out of sight. John watched for a few minutes longer before he left and went back to Anna's apartment building. He pulled his car behind the police car parked there and got out. The policeman sitting in the police car acknowledged John and rolled down his window.

"How's it been here?" John asked.

"Quiet," the policeman said.

"Good. It's okay. I'll take the watch from here. You go on home."

The policeman gave him a wave and drove off. John settled in his car and fought the sleep that wanted to settle over him. It was a long night.

Chapter 20

Anna?" Lisa remained in the doorway of the office, a slight tremor in her voice showing uncertainty about interrupting her employer.

"Yes?" Anna did not look up from the books in front of her.

"T-there's a man out here to see you."

"Who is it, Lisa?"

"A Mr. Kenneth Levall."

"Oh. Yes." Anna debated refusing to see him, but she had to continue as if she knew nothing until the police arrested him. "It's okay, Lisa. Show the senator in."

"Yes, ma'am."

"About time." Ken shoved his way past Lisa, almost knocking her down.

"Hello, Ken. I would say 'come in,' but you're already here."

Lisa rolled her eyes at Anna before she left and closed the door. Anna suppressed a smile and turned her attention back to Ken.

"What was the idea of keeping me waiting?" He seated himself without invitation, propping one leg on the other, resting an ankle on the opposite knee.

"Sorry about that. Lisa's new here. Anyway, I don't think you waited *that* long."

"It was longer than I should have waited, Anna."

"Don't be a snob, Ken. Anyway, I said I was sorry. What else do you want?" She slammed the ledger shut, got up from her chair, and put it in the top drawer of her filing cabinet. "Why are you here, Ken?"

"I just wanted to see you." Ken came up behind her and slid strong arms around her waist. He pulled her against him. She stiffened at his touch and tried to pull away from him. He tightened his arms around her, sliding one hand up to her breast, fondling it.

She pushed his hand away and tried to pry loose his grip on her.

"Dammit, now what's the matter?" Ken shoved her away from him, knocking her against the cabinet.

She whirled around to face him, her eyes ablaze with anger.

"The matter? You have the nerve to ask *me* what's the matter?" She trembled with anger, but the glint of amusement in his eyes at her outburst angered her even more. A red flush covered her face, and she stared, her eyes wide and unblinking. An overwhelming desire to hit him swept over her, but she knew he would only hit her back. *Now's not the time. Calm down. He likes getting you riled so don't give him the satisfaction. Just be patient. He'll get his in the end. Oh, yes, he'll get what he deserves. I'll see to that.*

"Surely you're not still mad about the delivery you made for me? My God, Anna, it's finished and done with. Get over it."

Rubbing the back of her neck, Anna turned away from Ken.

"No. No, I'm not still mad about that," she said through gritted teeth.

"Then what?"

"It's my sister, Ken."

Stepping away from her, he glanced back at the door. "Y-Your sister?" he stammered. "What's going on with her?"

"I found out yesterday she was murdered, Ken."

"I'm sorry to hear that."

"Yeah, me too."

"Do they know who did it?"

"They have their suspicions."

"Oh, who?"

You sorry bastard, you know who, and so do I.

"They're not telling me," she lied. "They just say they have a suspect."

"I see. Well, they'll find whoever did it, I'm sure."

Was that a trace of fear I heard in his voice? "Oh, yes, I'm very sure they will."

"Well, I'm sorry about your sister."

"Thanks."

He gently touched her cheek and kissed her. Without another word he left, closing the door behind him.

Anna gave a long sigh of relief and sat down behind her desk. She laid her head down on crossed arms and let the tears flow. She cried for her sister, for the loss of her love for Ken, and for herself. She did not hear the soft knock, nor the opening and closing of the door as Lisa peered at her. When all the tears had been shed and she felt emptied of all emotion, exhausted, Anna cleaned her face and left the store. She didn't say anything to Lisa but was well aware that her assistant watched her leave, a puzzled expression on her face.

She threw her purse onto the passenger seat and climbed into her car. She did not start her car but spent a few minutes with eyes closed and let the warmth of the sun soak into her body. Next Anna got her telephone out of her purse and dialed John's number. It rang several times before he answered.

"Mentz here."

"Hi."

"Anna. Are you all right?"

"Sure, I'm fine, I guess."

"What's up then?"

"I just needed to hear your voice."

"Where are you?"

"I'm just leaving the store. I couldn't stay there."

"Hey, I'm right here at a little hole in the wall called Pete's Corner. It's not far from you."

"Yes, I know where it's located."

"Meet me for a cup of coffee and a donut."

"Well..."

"Come on. It'll make my day. I could use a break and a beautiful woman to look at instead of my partner's ugly mug."

"Okay, I guess so. Give me five minutes to get there."

"See ya in a bit then."

Anna drove up in front of the diner exactly five minutes later and parked. She leaned forward, resting her forehead against the steering wheel. After a moment, she got out of her car and went in. The smell of coffee and French fries filled the air, and there were only a few people in the place. John rose halfway out of his seat and waved so Anna could see him.

She walked the length of the diner, conscientious of her red swollen eyes and the stares of the people she passed. She slid into the seat opposite the detective and gave him a weak smile.

"Are you sure you're okay?" he asked. "I can't help but notice how pale and tired you look."

"I'm fine. It's been a tough day." She was thankful he did not mention her puffy red eyes.

"What happened?"

"Ken came by the store. He was so … so sweet, in a way, and he tried to be comforting."

"Anna." John took her hands in his. "Don't fall into his trap again. Don't let his charisma fool you. It may get you killed. Don't you see what he's doing?"

She sighed. "I know you're right. I know you are."

"Would you like a cup of coffee?" he asked. "This place doesn't look like much, but the coffee is great."

"Yes, please."

"Anything to eat?"

"No, but thank you."

He signaled the waitress and ordered two coffees and two donuts.

"Now, what did he say or do? I need to know everything."

"There isn't that much to tell. I just told him about Tina's death, and he acted so sympathetic and caring. He seemed truly sorry to hear that she had died." She paused before whispering, "He seemed so caring."

The waitress placed a cup of coffee in front of John and one in front of Anna. The donuts were on the same plate and placed between them. Anna added sugar to her coffee. John took his coffee black. He offered a donut to her, but she shook her head at the offer. She sipped her coffee, her head down, refusing to meet his eyes.

"Anna, don't forget he is behind it all. Carl Blakely was hired by him to murder your sister." John swallowed back the jealous rage choking him.

"I know you're right." She frowned. "I guess he's good at acting, isn't he?"

"There's no guessing about it. We're gathering evidence now to put him away for a long time. He could even get the death penalty for Tina's murder."

"What do I do now?" A hint of uncertainty was reflected in her voice.

"What do you think?" He finished his coffee and donuts. He stood up and walked around to the side of her, leaned toward her, and kissed her. "I love you," he said in a low voice, "just in case you're interested."

* * *

"Are you sure you covered your tracks?" Ken's angered voice lashed out.

"Yes, I'm sure. I'm a pro at this, as you well know from past exploits," said Carl.

Ken looked around furtively, though they were in their usual place in the park. The small grove of trees and bushes hid them well from the view of the other people in the park.

"I don't know," Ken turned his attention back to Carl. "My feelings just aren't good about this. I think they are on to us, probably gathering evidence as we speak."

"I can kill her. No problem, though I may want to taste that sweet flesh of hers first. Drag it out a bit, ya know? Make her wish to die, maybe even beg for it." His laughter was chillingly wicked, and his eyes gleamed with the pleasure he was envisioning in his perverted mind.

Ken grabbed him by the shirt and pulled Carl's face close to his face. "You touch her, you son of a bitch, and I'll have your ass so quick you won't know what happened to you until it was too late. Do you understand?"

Carl's smug smile held a wickedness that sent shivers through Ken.

"I mean it, you God forsaken bastard. Don't you lay a hand on Anna. Have I made myself clear?"

"Yes, you have." Carl straightened his shirt. He turned and disappeared through the trees, not looking back.

"You better," Ken muttered under his breath, "or I'll kill you myself."

* * *

Anna was too tired to cook so she shoved a frozen dinner in the microwave. While it cooked, she poured a glass of wine. It didn't take long to eat her dinner and drink the wine. Afterward she curled up on the sofa. It was only a couple of days to her sister's funeral. It seemed most of her life had been about taking care of Tina and fighting for survival. What was left for her now? She leaned back and closed her eyes.

The doorbell rang. Her head jerked up and her body tensed. It rang again. Anna reluctantly got up, opened the door, and felt her heart in her throat.

"Hello, Anna," Ken said.

"Ken, I'm really tired and not up to company right now."

"I know. I won't come in."

"Then what are you doing here?"

"I just wanted to apologize for being so rude when I was at your shop today. That's all."

"Oh, okay. I appreciate your apology."

He reached out as if to grab her, but she stepped back just in time to avoid his grasp. When he looked at her with a hurt look, she realized for the first time she truly didn't care anymore. Not about him anyway. In fact, all she felt was an emptiness that hurt, and there was no way he could fill that void.

"Well, I guess I'll go. I do have work to do, and as you said, you're tired." He waited for her to say something, but she just looked coldly back at him. He bowed his head and turned to leave.

Anna closed the door firmly and locked it.

* * *

John watched the front door to Anna's apartment from his car, which was parked across the street. He had seen Ken go in the building. After debating whether or not to follow him, he decided to wait and see if he came out. It was not a long wait.

Ken exited the building about fifteen minutes after entering it. John breathed a sigh of relief, and then gave a slow grin. He watched as the senator got in his car and drove away. Without looking down, his hand reached for his cell phone on the seat next to him and flipped it open. John dialed Anna's number.

"Hello," she said in a voice filled with fatigue.

"Hey."

"Oh, John, it's you." She sounded relieved.

"Yeah, are you okay?"

"Uh huh, I'm just tired."

"Well, you've a right to be. I just called to wish you a goodnight."

"That is so sweet of you. Thanks."

He laughed. "I'm just full of sweetness."

"More than you know," she said in a soft voice.

There was a pause of silence. "Just keep thinking that, okay?"

"That's not a problem."

"Goodnight and sweet dreams."

"Night." She hung up.

John didn't hang up until a moment after Anna had. *She sounds exhausted. I sure hope she can hold up until we see this all the way through. So close, we're so close.*

Chapter 21

Anna closed her eyes and listened to the rain beating against the tent that covered the grave site. The minister's voice droned on as someone behind her cried audibly. Anna tried to concentrate on the sweet smell of the flowers to help forget her sister was gone. It was hard to accept the loss of Tina, and her anger boiled just below the surface.

More than half the people present Anna didn't know. She assumed they were friends of Tina's, maybe even some had worked with her sister. It was comforting to Anna that people thought enough of Tina to attend the funeral despite the rain.

After the service, she stood stiffly as the people filed by, voicing their condolences. She forced a weak smile and thanked each for being there.

Finally alone, Anna turned to watch the casket lowered into the grave. The rain slowed to a drizzle. She felt empty and numb. Memories of her parents' funeral came flooding back, and a sob escaped her controlled demeanor.

"Are you okay?" The voice startled her, and she whirled around.

"I'll be okay, Ken, thanks."

"Is there anything I can do for you?"

"No thanks." She turned from him. A movement in the small group of people who lingered caught her eye. She strained to see, sure she had seen the man who had come to her shop. But when the group parted, as people left, there was no sign of him.

When Anna looked back, Ken was walking toward his car. She breathed a sigh of relief. She just couldn't deal with him, couldn't pretend she cared. Not today, maybe not ever.

"Anna, let's go home." Lisa took her arm and led her to the limousine. The ride home was quiet. When they arrived at the apartment, Lisa sat her on the sofa, wrapped an afghan around her, and, after making two cups of hot tea, joined her.

"You know you're welcome to stay with me for however long you need," Lisa said.

"Thanks, Lisa. I'll just stay here. But if you don't mind, I'm going to stay away from the shop for a few days."

"Hey, take as long as you need, Anna. I can handle it."

"Thanks." Anna reached out and placed her hand over Lisa's.

The doorbell rang. Anna moaned and said, "I can't handle company right now."

"I'll get rid of them." Lisa hurried to the door and opened it. There was some muffled talk, and the door was closed.

"Who was…." Anna turned.

John stood inside. When she saw him, she burst into tears. He quickly sat beside her and gathered her into his arms. He didn't say a word but held her and let her cry. She cried until she fell asleep. He continued to hold her.

Chapter 22

Anna inserted her key in the apartment door and stood still as the door swung open, the funeral from a week ago still fresh in her mind. Memories of her sister's apartment could not be forgotten and an eerie chill went through her. Flashbacks continued to haunt her. She quickly flipped on the hall light before shutting the door behind her, and her dark mood was uplifted at the familiar sight of her living room with everything neatly in place. After turning on the lamps, she opened the drapes to expose the doors that led to the balcony. Soft music flowed from the stereo as she poured a glass of wine and stepped onto the balcony. The night lights of the city created a halo of light in the sky. The street below filled with cars, their drivers intent on their destinations. This was her favorite time of the day. She sat down in a lounge chair and took it all in.

The daylight faded and darkness crept close. Anna closed her eyes and allowed the soft music to wrap her in its arms while a cool breeze ruffled through her hair. Gradually she felt her body release its tension. Stress had dominated her life ever since her parents died. She almost forgot what it was like to not worry about something, but at this moment, for just a moment, she shoved it all out of her mind.

Feeling better she undressed, took a long, hot shower and put on pink pajamas and a matching robe. She made a ham and cheese sandwich to satisfy her nagging hunger and curled up on the sofa with a magazine and a second glass of wine. The doorbell rang, and she rose to answer it. With her hand on the doorknob, she hesitated and put her eye to the peephole. There was no one there.

What the heck? Frowning in exasperation, she turned to go back to her magazine and wine when the doorbell rang again. *Darn! I might as well answer it. Whoever it is isn't going to let me have any peace.* When Anna opened the door, Carl Blakely stood in front of her, dressed all in black. He had one hand shoved in the pocket of his black leather jacket.

"Hi," he said, grinning at her.

"Oh." Her voice was flat with displeasure. "Hello." She stepped back and partially shut the door.

"Just thought I would drop by and see ya." Carl put his foot against the door to block her from totally closing it.

"Well, I appreciate that." She felt trapped, and her mind raced furiously to find a way to get rid of him without raising his suspicions. "But I'm not really in the mood to entertain tonight. I'm very tired."

"I won't be long."

"No, I'll give you a call." She tried to put a confident firmness in her voice, and then a thought occurred to her. "By the way, how did you get my address?"

"That girl who works at your store gave it to me. She said you'd love to see me."

"No, there's no way she'd give you my address." Suspicion edged her voice.

He put his hand against the door and gently pushed against it.

"No!" Anna cried as she shoved hard against the door with her body.

He pushed with more force, knocking her back. She turned to run to the bedroom, but he grabbed her. She cried out and struggled to free herself. He yelped as she dug her fingernails into his arm, drawing blood. A loud noise came from behind them, and Anna heard Carl groan. There was a scrambling of feet and grunts behind her, and she felt the release of Carl's grip on her. She fell to the floor. More scuffling came from behind her as she picked herself up. Glancing over her shoulder, she saw two men wrestling Carl Blakely to the floor. One held him down while the other handcuffed his wrists.

"Thank God," she whispered. Someone grabbed her by the shoulders and for a moment fear rose into her throat, but when she turned around and looked, she threw her arms around John's neck.

"Are you all right?" He said, his eyes filled with concern.

"I am now." She pushed a stray curl back from her face.

"Did he hurt you?"

"Other than scaring me to death? No, I'm fine."

"He won't scare you or bother you in any way again. He's going to jail for the murder of your sister."

"Good."

"I think the DNA under Tina's fingernails will match his. No chance in hell he'll get out of this."

"How did you know he was here?" She said.

"I had a policeman watching you and another one watching your apartment. They called me as soon as they saw him wandering around the neighborhood. Since he made that little visit to your store, I was concerned he would go even further and follow you or visit your apartment. I was right."

"I'm so glad." She laughed nervously.

"Me, too. He might have killed you."

"John?"

"Yeah."

"Do you think Ken sent him to kill me?"

"I'm not sure. It's a possibility, though. We'll interrogate him. Hopefully, we'll find out a lot of useful information that will help with our case. Then we'll make more arrests."

"Okay."

"Will you be all right here by yourself?"

"I think so."

"I'll have a policeman guarding your door. If you need anything, tell him."

"Thanks, I will."

He gave her a quick kiss on top of her nose and held her close to him, looking into her eyes.

"This will all be finished eventually," he promised.

"I know. It just won't be soon enough for me."

He gave an understanding nod and left, closing the door gently behind him.

Chapter 23

The next morning the phone rang as she dressed for work. She grabbed the hand set and answered. “Hello?”

“Good morning.” John sounded tired. “How are you this morning?”

“I’m okay. Didn’t sleep much, I’m afraid.”

“Neither did I. I was up most of the night interrogating your intruder from last night.”

“Oh? How'd that go?”

“Well, it was a tough night, but I just thought it would make you feel better to know that the senator didn’t send him to your apartment. He did that on his own. He claims the senator didn’t tell him to kill you. In fact, he was ordered to keep his hands off of you unless the senator told him different.”

She gave a sigh of relief.

“However,” John continued, “the senator did hire him to kill Tina.”

“I see. Did he tell you why?”

“She was digging up too much shit on the senator, and he was afraid she would expose him.”

“I see.”

“Listen, I’m tired, and I’ve got a few things yet to do. I’ll see you tonight, okay?”

Anna smiled. “That’ll be fine. I’ll be here.”

* * *

That evening the doorbell rang, and Anna opened the door to see John standing outside.

"Hi." John leaned against the doorframe. He looked tired, his face drawn and eyes bloodshot.

"Hi there, come in." Her eyes were red, make-up streaks ran down her cheeks.

"Are you okay?" He stepped inside the apartment and shut the door.

"I will be."

"Why're you crying? For Tina?"

"Partly, but ... I don't know. I guess everything hit me all at once, and I had to release some of the stress, the tension, the pain. It's all been like a bad dream, and I keep wondering when I'm going to wake up."

He held her against him and rubbed her back until he felt the weight of her body relax against him. He buried his face in her neck, breathing in the soft aroma of her perfume. She wrapped her arms around his neck in quiet acceptance as her body arched towards him. A soft sigh escaped her lips.

The doorbell rang, and Anna gave a startled jerk. She brushed a dark curl back from her face and glanced at John, their eyes met in silent questioning.

"Expecting someone else?" He asked.

"No, not at all."

"Answer it," he said, his arms loosened from around her.

"But what if ..."

"Don't worry about that. If it's him, we'll deal with it, okay?"

"Okay." Her voice didn't sound confident, but she walked to the door and reached for the door handle. She paused for a moment and glanced back just in time to see the bedroom door close. She opened the door and looked into the familiar green eyes of Senator Kenneth Levall. A gold-flecked green tie hung partially loosened around his neck, his face drawn and unsmiling.

"I couldn't open the door with my key. What's the deal with that?"

"I had the lock changed."

"Oh, really?"

The sarcasm in his voice ignited her anger, and she struggled to suppress it. She didn't answer his comment and just waited to see what he would say or do.

"I've missed you." His voice was not convincing. "Where have you been?"

"I've, uh, been around."

"Really? Sure about that?" He stepped inside and gave the door a shove. His arms slipped around her and his mouth covered her full lips. Her arms at her side, she stiffened. He let go of her, a puzzled look on his face. "What's the matter?"

"Nothing." She turned and walked towards the bar. "Would you like something to drink?"

The sound of his footsteps followed her, but Anna kept her back to him. Afraid to look at him, afraid he would see the hate she felt for him, the distrust, she reached for the wine glasses when she felt his hands on her shoulders. She gasped and cringed away from him.

"No," he said, "I don't want anything to drink. I just …." He paused as if he heard the pleading in his own voice.

"What do you want from me, Ken?" *No, don't let him get to you. Don't give in to him again. Don't weaken. He killed Tina. He's a monster.*

"I want you back." He shifted her to face him.

"I can't, Ken. It's finished between us."

"It's him, isn't it?"

"What do you mean?"

"You're in love with him, aren't you?"

"I don't know what you're talking about." Anna tried to push him away so she wouldn't have to look at him, see any hurt in his eyes, any pain on his face, but his hands held her firmly.

"Tell me the truth, Anna."

She averted her eyes so he couldn't see the confusion, the yearning, or the repulsion she felt. If he knew she knew... She couldn't take the chance of him knowing. *Why isn't he in jail?*

Gathering her courage, she stated, "It's none of your business."

"Damn it, Anna, how could you? How long has the affair been going on?"

She glanced at him. *How can I see pain in his eyes? He doesn't really care.* She quickly twisted her head away and said, "I don't know what you're talking about, Ken. I'm not having an affair with John. He rescued me from a dangerous situation. We've become very good friends, that's all."

"Friends? Yeah, sure." His voice dripped with sarcastic disbelief.

"Ken, don't do this."

"You belong to me. Remember that."

Anna jerked around to glare at him. "I'm not your possession."

"Oh, really? You bitch. I made you what you are. I did more for you than anyone," he said. "You *are* my possession." He reached and slipped his hand under the pendant she wore. "I even gave you diamonds. I remember how happy you were when I put this necklace around your neck." He lowered his hand and sneered at her. "Your policeman friend wouldn't be that generous with you."

She pushed past him. "I can't believe I loved you," she said. He grabbed her arm and pulled her around to face him. She pulled free of his hold, felt the anger inside rise to the surface—boil to the surface—until she couldn't be quiet any longer.

"Yes, Ken, you gave me everything," Anna said through gritted teeth. "You gave me this nice apartment, decorated to *your* taste. You provided me with a monthly allowance for my needs until I got back on my feet." The bitterness in her voice couldn't be contained.

"A very generous allowance, Anna."

"Oh, yes, I admit that it is, and a credit card with a limit on it I'll never in a million years reach. That doesn't fill the emptiness." She put her hand on her chest, her eyes ablaze with emotion. "I have other needs, Ken. What about them?" Her voice rose to a crescendo. Tears welled up in her eyes, filling them until they spilled onto her face. "You bought me once, but you'll never do it again."

"Anna." His voice softened.

"And I miss Tina."

"Your sister's dead. She's not coming back. You might as well accept that fact."

"I know. You killed her." *There! It's out.*

"No. No, Anna, I didn't. I wouldn't do that. I love you, Anna. You ought to know that."

"Know that? How? I'm your mistress, your possession, nothing more. That's not love, Ken. And not only that, if you loved me, you wouldn't have me delivering your drug money." She drew in a deep breath, eyes ablaze with anger she couldn't hold back any longer.

Ken stood silent, his eyes glued to her. After a moment, he said in a soft voice, "I chose you to make those deliveries, Anna, because you were the only one I trusted to do it."

Her expression softened as she absorbed what he just said. He reached out as if to take her hand, but she made no move to take it.

"He used you." A voice responded from the shadows of the bedroom. John stepped into the light.

Ken shifted his attention toward John. "Used her? I think it's more that she used me. I'm the one who saved her ass when she had nothing and no place to go." He rubbed his hand across his brow. "What are you doing here?"

"He's here with me," Anna answered.

"Oh?" He turned back to her, eyes blazing. "Did you make love to him in the same bed where we once made love?"

"No!"

"Damn it, Anna, don't lie to me." Ken's lips tightened, his eyes narrowed, and his hands balled into fists. He eased his right hand inside his jacket and stepped toward her. Anna backed away from him, from the crazed look in his eyes. She gasped and looked at John, her eyes wide, afraid.

A glint of light reflected from Ken's hand as it emerged from his jacket. He pointed the gun at her as he rushed toward her and grabbed her wrist. She pulled against his strength, raised her other hand, and brought her fist down hard across the bridge of his nose. With a grunt of pain, he loosened his grip on her. Anna's shoulder bumped against his hand, and the gun clattered to the floor and slid a short distance away. A quick step brought Anna close enough to pick it up. The gun in her hand, she whirled to face the senator. Her cold, hard eyes held the disdain she felt.

His hand covered his nose while blood seeped between his fingers. She raised the gun and pointed it toward him. The senator's face paled when he heard the click of the safety being released and watched with wide eyes as she cocked the gun. He lowered his hand from his nose, and his mouth dropped open. A pool of blood dribbled from his nose onto his upper lip. Over the barrel of the gun, she watched it linger there for a moment.

"Anna, don't!" He cringed back from her.

The drop of blood made its way down his upper lip to the opening of his mouth. His tongue wiped it away, but he still reached up to wipe the blood from his nose. His eyes grew wide as he looked up at her, and he shook his head as she took aim.

"No, don't. Please," he begged. "I love you, Anna. Please. Think about what you're about to do." He held his hands up in supplication.

"This is for Tina," she replied.

"No, Anna!" John lunged toward her.

His arms came around her from behind, and she was vaguely aware of the warmth of his body against her back. His hand reached around, fingers opened wide. His arm bumped against her arm, but before he could wrap his hand around her hand, her arm jerked. A shot reverberated through the air.

Ken looked at her in disbelief. His mouth opened and shut, but he didn't utter a sound.

John released his grip, and the gun hit the floor with a clatter. He took a step back. Anna wrapped her arms around her waist, while the room spun. Unaware of the trembling of her body, she bent forward and covered her face with her hands as nausea filled her throat.

The senator slowly dropped to his knees, a spreading stain turning his white shirt a bright red. Then his body crumpled to the floor, and his blank eyes stared at the ceiling unseeing.

John stared in disbelief at the two people before him. Then his eyes narrowed and his hands clenched into white-knuckled fists. Horror covered his face.

"My God," he said. "Oh, my God."

Chapter 24

nna lowered the newspaper slowly and sat staring at the headline.

UNDERCOVER AGENT CONFESSES TO THE MURDER OF SENATOR KENNETH LEVALL

"I can't believe this," she said. "Why did he do this?"

She pulled out the telephone book and looked up the number for Davis, Steadman, and Carroll, Attorneys at Law. With the tip of her pen she dialed the number and waited for an answer.

"Hello, I'm Anna Kayce, and I'd like to speak with Mr. Davis, please. It's concerning the John Mentz case, and it's important." She waited while on hold.

"Hello again," she said and then listened. "Yes, I can come over right now. Okay, thanks." Anna hung up the phone, grabbed her jacket and purse, and left the store, waving at Lisa as she went out the door.

It only took her fifteen minutes to get to the lawyer's office. As she got out of the car, a moment of doubt struck her, but she shook it off and entered the office of Larry Davis.

She looked around, surprised at what she saw. There was a burgundy leather sofa and a wing-backed chair. Various other chairs were scattered around the room with the usual tables, lamps, and magazines. The room was carpeted with a navy plush weave that muffled the sounds of people moving around in the room. It was a very professional surrounding and yet very comfortable. To top it all off, there was the sound of soft music in the background. A blond head popped up from behind a glass window and gave her a very attractive and sweet smile.

"Yes, ma'am, may I help you?" The voice matched the smile.

"I'm Anna Kayce."

"Oh, yes, he's expecting you. Have a seat, and Mr. Davis will be with you shortly." The blond head disappeared.

Anna sat on the burgundy chair and tried to ignore the butterflies in the pit of her stomach. True to the receptionist's word, she didn't wait long before she was ushered into a large office with walls that were filled with law books.

"Good morning, Ms. Kayce." Tall and thin, Davis was a handsome man despite his hard, angular features. His hair was sprinkled lightly with gray which gave him a distinguished appearance against the navy blue suit and white shirt he wore.

Anna smiled and held out her hand as she walked toward his desk. His handshake was firm. Gray eyes bore into her, and she was aware he was assessing her. She squared her shoulders and met his gaze straight on.

"Hello. Please, just call me Anna."

"Okay, Anna, have a seat and tell me what's on your mind." He waited until she was seated before he sank into the plush leather chair behind him.

"I, uh, I saw in the newspaper that John confessed to murdering Ken."

"Yes," Davis said, "against my advice he did confess."

"Why?" She grasped the edge of the desk with one hand and turned pleading eyes toward him.

"Well, I'm really not prepared to discuss the case with you. John is out on bail at the moment. You could try asking him to answer that question for you."

"Oh, okay." She seemed uncertain about what to do but stood up and held out her hand. "Thank you for taking the time with me."

He took her hand and held it, preventing her from leaving.

"I wonder if I could ask you a question or two?" He said.

"Well, sure." She took her hand back from him and sat down again.

"When the gun went off, did you pull the trigger?"

"No!"

"Did John have his finger over yours and could he have pushed your finger against the trigger?"

"Why are you asking these questions?" She frowned, her tone demanding.

Attorney Davis walked around the desk and sat on the edge of it. His expression was thoughtful, and after a moment of silence, he spoke.

"I'll be honest with you, Anna. I'm at a bit of a loss as to how to defend John, and he hasn't made it any easier by confessing."

"But, Mr. Davis, I promise you he didn't do it. That's why I don't understand why he confessed."

Another hesitation. "I haven't had a chance to discuss it with him, Anna, but it's my feeling he did it to protect you."

"Oh, my God, no." Horror crossed over her face. "I've got to talk to him right away." She half stood when he held his hand up to stop her.

"Wait," he said.

She sat down and looked at him expectantly.

"He can take back his confession, but it doesn't guarantee they'll drop the charges. More than likely they'll turn around and charge you as well for murder. They're probably going to anyway."

"Mr. Davis, I don't know how to prove it, but that gun went off of its own accord when John bumped my arm."

He nodded at her, rolling his lips in. "Okay, I'll work on that angle." He gave her a reassuring smile and took the hand she offered him.

"I'm counting on that. John's counting on it, too." She left his office.

* * *

Anna drove aimlessly around for a while. The whole thing had been pushed as far back in her mind as she could push it. Now she was pulling it out and laying it all out to look at once again, to relive it, to analyze each horrible moment.

When she was through, she pulled her car to the curb, turned the motor off, and leaned her head against the steering wheel. Exhaustion weighed heavily on her. After a short while, she started the car, looked around to see where she was, and, realizing she was close to where John lived, drove to his apartment.

Anna pulled the car up to the curb in front of the apartment and turned off the motor. She sat for a moment and looked around. The yard was mowed but drab. A flower pot lay on its side at the foot of the steps. Dirt had spilled out, and there were signs of a dried up brown flower amongst the debris. She did not discern any signs of life coming from the apartment but got out of the car and walked to the door anyway. She hesitated a moment before pressing the doorbell. A few minutes passed before she turned to leave. The door opened, and John stood in the doorway. He was pale and drawn. The dark circles under his eyes told her he was not sleeping. It pained her to see him like this, but she forced a smile. He didn't return it.

"Hi," she said.

"Hey."

The silence lengthened between them. Anna found herself uncertain as to what to say to John. She rubbed her sweaty palms together as her mind worked furiously to think of how to proceed.

"Why don't you come in, Anna." he finally said, standing aside to allow her to get by him.

"Thanks." She stepped into his apartment. It was her first time there so, curious, she looked around. It was simple and surprisingly neat. The drapes were drawn, making it dim inside and was the only sign of John's depression other than the lack-luster look in his eyes which alarmed her. She sat on the edge of the sofa and hugged her purse against her chest, not sure how to proceed.

"You look good, Anna," John said as he sat in a chair opposite her. "What are you doing here?"

"I saw in the newspapers that you confessed to killing Ken. Why, John? You and I both know you didn't do any such thing."

John looked down at his hands and didn't answer right away. She waited.

"I, uh, confessed because I felt responsible for the gun going off, Anna." He looked up, and it pained her to see defeat in his eyes.

"No, John, you weren't responsible. Neither of us was responsible. It just happened."

"If I had not…" He paused.

Anna watched him, watched the struggle that was going on inside of him, watched as his spirit slowly died, watched as the man she had come to love changed into someone she didn't know.

"John, if you had not tried to stop me, I'd never have pulled that trigger. I just would not have done it, and you did not pull the trigger. It was just a freak accident. Don't you understand?" Her voice took on a pleading tone.

"I know you believe that, but I just don't see it the same way as you do." John turned his hands palms outward.

"Obviously you don't, but you're looking at it all wrong. I just don't know how to explain it any better."

He stood up and started pacing around the room. After a few minutes he stopped the pacing and sat down again. The look on his face told her what she needed to know.

"Oh, my God! You think I really did pull that trigger, and you're taking the blame for me. You are, aren't you?" She brought her hands to her face. "I can't believe this. How could you?"

John turned his head away from her. He made no effort to deny her accusation. As if to get away, he stood up and went into the kitchen. Soon there was a sound of running water and the rattling of dishes. As Anna composed herself, the aroma of fresh brewed coffee reached her. John came back to the living room carrying a tray loaded with cups, sugar, spoons, and a carafe of coffee. Without saying anything, he poured the coffee, stirred in sugar, and handed it to her. He took his coffee black. Sitting back in his chair, he took a sip of the hot liquid and settled his gaze upon her.

"Is it okay?" He asked, raising one eyebrow.

"No, it's not okay, John. You can't do this."

"I meant the coffee, Anna."

"Oh, sorry."

"It's okay."

"Yes, it's fine, thanks," she said in a calmer voice. She leaned back and let the warmth fill her. "I'm sorry. I shouldn't have come on so strong, shouldn't have let myself get so upset. It's just that I can't believe you're doing this."

"It's nothing for you to worry about," he said. "I do understand."

Anna went to him and knelt at his feet. She took his hand in hers. "John, I love you. I don't want to lose you this way. I promise you I did not kill Ken, and I know you didn't either. You've got to take your confession back."

"I guess it's not clear to you, Anna. I could do what you just suggested, but they'll still think I did it. I'll still go on trial for murder." He hesitated. "And so will you."

"Well, then there's only one thing left to do. I'll go to the police and tell them I did it, not you."

John laughed. "That won't solve the problem, Anna, but thanks for the gesture."

"Why won't it work?"

"Because, my dear, they will just think we were in cahoots and charge us both." He leaned forward and kissed her on the nose. "No, you just stay out of it for now. Anyway, I can't guarantee they won't charge you. I get the feeling the prosecutor thinks we were in this together." He frowned. "I sure hope I'm wrong about that."

Her face fell. He took her hand and pulled her up and into his lap. She laid her head on his shoulder and sighed.

"I guess it's hopeless, huh?" She said.

"I don't know. I guess it would be best if we just expect the worse."

"I really got us into a mess, and I don't know how to get us out of it, but I refuse to do anything but think positive about this." She looked at him. He stared straight ahead with unseeing eyes.

His silence worried her.

* * *

Anna shifted her purse to her other hand in order to unlock her apartment door. She could not get the key to turn in the lock so she pulled it out and looked at it.

"Darn, it's the wrong key," she mumbled to herself. After fumbling with the keys in her hand, she found the right key and pushed it into the lock. A rustling sound startled her, and she whirled around. He was a small man with thick glasses on his face. He grinned at her.

"I didn't mean to scare you," he said in a whiny voice.

"What do you want?" Her irritation showed in her voice.

"Are you Anna Kayce?"

"Why do you want to know?"

He shoved his hand in his pocket. This scared her, and she turned back to unlocking her door. When she opened it, she quickly went inside and turned to close the door. He was in the doorway, holding an envelope out to her.

"What is this?" She said with caution.

"You're being served, Ms. Kayce." He gave a little salute when she took the envelope from his hand. "Have a great day." With a quick nod he turned and left her standing there, mouth open in disbelief.

Anna closed the door and laid her purse on the table next to the doorway. She sat down on the sofa, looking at the envelope. It took a moment before she got the nerve up to open and read it. When through reading, she laid it down on the sofa beside her.

"I can't believe this. It just can't be true." Anna leaned forward, hands over her mouth, eyes closed. There were no more tears left. When she sat up, she reached for the phone, dialed a number, and waited for an answer on the other end.

"Mr. Davis? This is Anna. I thought I ought to tell you I've been subpoenaed to be a witness for the prosecution."

Chapter 25

Wednesday, April 10, 2002

"Your Honor, the prosecution would like to call Dr. David Mercer." Prosecutor Hawthorne stayed behind the table, both hands resting on the back of a chair. He did not glance back at the bald, dumpy-looking man who entered the courtroom. After being sworn in, Dr. Mercer sat in the witness chair.

"State your name, address, and occupation for the court, please."

"Dr. David Mercer, seventy-one Michaels Lane, Daylan, North Carolina. I'm a criminologist and forensics scientist, specializing in weapons," he stated with an air of confidence.

"With which facility are you associated?"

"The Cranston Forensics Laboratory."

"How long have you been in the field?"

"Thirty years, sir."

The prosecutor smiled as he walked around the table, which placed him in front of the jury box.

"Thirty years. That's a long time. Have you ever testified as an expert witness before?"

"More times than I can count."

"I believe you said you specialized in weapons."

"Yes, sir."

"And you are familiar with the Smith & Wesson .38 Special?"

"Yes, sir."

Prosecutor Hawthorne walked to the evidence table and picked up a plastic bag containing a revolver.

"Your Honor, Exhibit A has already been submitted into evidence."

"Proceed with your questioning," said the judge.

"Dr. Mercer, this is the gun found at the scene of the crime." He handed the plastic bag containing the gun to the witness. "Can you identify it, please?"

"Yes, I can. It's a Smith & Wesson .38 Special."

"We have already introduced the ballistics report proving it to be the murder weapon." The prosecutor paused and looked at the defense lawyer as if expecting an objection.

"The defense has no objection to this, You Honor," Defense Attorney Davis said.

Prosecutor Hawthorne turned back to the witness. "Look at the weapon, please, and tell me about this gun."

"Well, it appears to be a Smith & Wesson .38 Special, double action, short barrel that fires six rounds. It would be easy to conceal on one's person. This particular gun only weighs about 13.5 ounces fully loaded."

"When you say double action, what does that mean?"

"It means if it is not cocked first, it has a longer pull distance to cock the hammer and discharge of the gun."

"Longer distance?"

"Yes, in other words it takes longer to fire the weapon because you have to cock it first before discharging the bullet. If it were manually cocked before pulling the trigger, then it doesn't take as long to discharge."

"I see. Tell me, Dr. Mercer, would the trigger on this gun be more sensitive if it were cocked first?"

"Yes."

"In your opinion, Dr. Mercer, could this gun have gone off accidentally when Detective Mentz grabbed it."

"In my opinion, no."

"Why do you say that?"

"A trained professional such as Detective Mentz would have pushed the gun away from the victim rather than trying to grab it. Not only that, he would have had to knock it hard to cause it to discharge. It's my understanding he only bumped Ms. Kayce's arm."

"Thank you, Dr. Mercer, I have no more questions." He turned away from the witness and looked at the defense lawyer. "Your witness."

Davis did not get up immediately, taking a moment to look at the piece of paper lying on the table in front of him. The murmuring which filled the courtroom faded into complete silence before he looked up. Slowly rising from his chair, he walked to the witness stand. He bowed his head just slightly, acknowledging the witness before him, and turned to the judge.

"Your Honor, I have no questions of this witness at the moment, but I would like to reserve the right to question later."

The prosecutor glanced up from the notes in front of him, a surprised look on his face. Someone in the courtroom gasped. A low rumbling wafted through the room, and the judge banged his gavel for silence.

"I want quiet in this courtroom," the judge warned, "or I will clear it and allow no one inside." The room grew quiet. "I will not tolerate any further outburst like this."

"Mr. Davis, are you sure you are serving your client's best interest by not questioning Dr. Mercer at this time?" The judge said.

"Yes, sir, but as I requested, I reserve the right to recall him later."

"Request granted. You may step down from the witness stand, Dr. Mercer, but you must remain available for further questioning if necessary. Mr. Prosecutor, do you have any more witnesses at this time?"

"No, Your Honor, the prosecution rests its case at this time."

"Mr. Davis, the floor is yours. You may call your first witness."

"Your Honor, I would appreciate a fifteen minute break to confer with my client before proceeding," Defense Attorney Davis said.

"Granted. Court will break for fifteen minutes," Judge Claudell pounded his gavel in dismissal.

Chapter 26

"Okay, John, let's talk." Davis occupied a chair across the conference room table from John. "I don't have much to work with here. Their case is based on circumstantial evidence. That's the good news. It's basically your word against theirs. Is there anything that you haven't told me, anything at all?"

"I can't think of anything."

"Okay, if that's the case, then it is up to our expert witness to convince the jurors."

"What do you think our chances are to win this?"

"Chances? At best, I'd say fifty-fifty."

"I see," John said, running his fingers through his hair.

"John?"

"Yeah."

"You didn't pull that trigger, did you?"

John sighed, taking a moment before answering. "I admit for just one quick second I considered it, but no, I didn't."

"What about Anna? Did she?"

John looked away and ran his hand over his face.

"You think she did it, don't you?" Davis said.

"No! No, I don't. I think, like me, she thought about it, but if she were going to kill him, she would've pulled that trigger sooner. No, I think when it got right down to it, she couldn't do it."

"Okay, that's a good point."

"It's just that..."

"What?"

"I still feel that I caused the gun to go off when I tried to push the gun away from the line of fire. It was my fault."

"John, that could very well be what happened, but then it would be considered an accident." Davis looked at John thoughtfully, tapping his chin with his forefinger. "Tell me something, John."

"What?"

"Once again, do you believe deep inside of you that Anna deliberately pulled the trigger?"

John hesitated as his eyes shifted to his left.

"I see," the attorney said.

"No!" John's eyes blazed with anger, and he clenched his fists. His voice grew louder. "She was angry, yes. She was hurt—deeply hurt. But no, when it got right down to it, she couldn't—wouldn't—do it. Otherwise, she would've pulled that trigger long before it happened. She would have."

"Tell me why, then, did she cock that gun?"

John sat quiet for a moment before he quietly replied, "I don't know."

"I see. Do you think her capable of tricking someone else into killing the senator?"

John looked at his attorney in disbelief, a frown on his face. "I... I can't believe you would even think that. No, she wouldn't. Not only that, but I couldn't be deceived like that. I would've known what she was doing. She was scared of him, afraid he was going to kill her."

"Okay, okay. Just calm down. I have to consider all possibilities."

"Yeah."

"Do you love her enough to lie for her?"

John looked his attorney in the eyes, his gaze steady and unmoving. "No," he said firmly.

Attorney Davis pressed his lips together, rolling the lower lip inward and stood up, squaring his shoulders.

"Then let's go and fight for justice."

Chapter 27

"Your Honor, I would like to call my next witness, Detective John Mentz." Defense Attorney Davis turned and looked at John. A rustling stirred through the courtroom when John rose from his seat, but this quieted as he walked to the witness stand and was sworn in.

"State your full name, address, and occupation for the court, please." Davis said.

"My name is Detective John Edward Mentz. I live at 615 Broad Street, apartment number 315 and am a law enforcement officer with the Daylan City Police Department."

"What specifically is your capacity with the police department?"

"I'm an undercover agent with the Drug and Alcohol Division."

"I see. Were you investigating Senator Kenneth Levall in this capacity?"

"Yes."

"What were your findings?"

"He was the kingpin of a big drug ring that covered most of the state. He also had connections in Florida and Mexico and was making negotiations to expand to South America."

"You were aware of his relationship with Anna Kayce, is that correct?"

"Yes, she told me."

"She told you?" Davis raised an eyebrow. "You didn't know before you met her that night in the alley?"

"I knew of her, but I didn't realize that was her that night in the alley until I ran a check on her license plate."

"When did you realize she may have something to do with the drug operation the senator was running?"

"It was the first time we went out to dinner. We talked, and as she talked about herself, I began to become suspicious that she was involved, and yet I had the feeling that she was unaware of what she was actually doing when she made the deliveries."

Davis glanced toward the jury and took notice of their rapt attention. He turned back to John and continued his interrogation.

"You also know that Anna believed the senator was behind the murder of her sister?" Davis said.

"Yes, I'm aware of that."

"You were developing a relationship with Anna, were you not?"

"I, uh, guess you could say that."

"Was it an intimate relationship?"

"No."

"Are you in love with her?"

John slid his glance toward the jury and down to the floor. "Yes, I am."

"Do you love her enough to cover up if she committed murder?"

"No! No way would I do that."

"Enough to commit murder for her?"

"No!" His voice grew louder, and he looked at the jurors. "There's no way I would or could do that."

Davis held his hand up as if to bring things to a halt.

"Okay, Detective Mentz, tell me one more thing. Dr. Mercer testified that a trained professional such as you would have pushed the gun away from the victim rather than grabbing the gun. Is this true?"

"Yes, and that is what I was trying to do. But the gun went off when my hand touched hers. I barely touched her hand." He turned pleading eyes to the jurors. "It happened so fast I didn't have time to push her hand holding the gun away from the senator."

"Detective Mentz, did you murder Senator Levall?"

"No, I did not." His voice was firm and confident.

"You confessed to this murder. Why?"

"I thought it was a possibility at first that I had caused the gun to go off without realizing it. Everything happened so fast."

"John, were you also covering for Anna?"

John bowed his head without speaking.

"John?" Davis said gently.

"I wasn't so much covering for Anna because I thought she had done it as I was afraid she would be charged for murder. I never believed she pulled that trigger, but I thought she would be charged with murder." His voice was low but became louder as he spoke. John looked at the jury as if imploring them to believe him.

"Thank you, John." Davis turned to the prosecutor. "Your witness."

* * *

The prosecutor walked with slow steps to the witness stand and looked at John, his face solemn. He cleared his throat. The already thick tension in the room grew even thicker.

"Detective Mentz, you were shot by someone you believed to be Senator Levall, were you not?"

"Yes, I was."

"Where did this occur?"

John wiggled around uncomfortably in his seat before saying, "The incident occurred in front of Anna's apartment building."

"You had spent the evening with Anna, had you not?"

"Yes, we had dinner together."

"Did the senator come to the apartment while you were there?"

"No, no, he didn't. When I left the building and was about to get in my car, a shot grazed my shoulder." John threw a quick glance toward Anna.

"So, how did you come to the conclusion the senator was the one responsible?"

"I saw his car parked down the street in a dark area. When I drove away and turned the car around, I parked in a position where I could watch the car. It wasn't long until I saw a man get into that car. I believed then and I believe now it was him."

"That gave you reason to have a personal vendetta against the senator, correct?"

"It gave me reason, but I didn't have a personal vendetta against him." John glared at the prosecutor.

"The senator still had the love and loyalty of the woman you wanted, Detective Mentz. Then someone you believed to be the senator shoots you. Sounds like you had every reason to seek revenge."

"Objection." The defense attorney jumped from his chair.

"Sustained," said the judge.

"Thank you, Detective Mentz, no more questions." The prosecutor's face displayed a pleased smile. He had made his point.

The judge turned to John and said, "You may step down from the witness stand, Detective Mentz."

* * *

"Your Honor, I would like to call Anna Kayce back to the stand, please," the defense attorney said.

"Anna Kayce, please take the stand." The bailiff said.

Already sworn in, Anna took her place in the witness stand. Her drawn face appeared starkly pallid against the navy blue suit she wore. She sat with back straight and shoulders squared. With chin uplifted, she unswervingly met the stares of the jurors.

"Anna, you testified earlier that you had a personal relationship with the senator that was also a business relationship. Is that correct?"

"Yes."

"Then you discovered that he had been using you for drug payoffs?"

"That is correct."

"And it was after that your sister was murdered?"

"He had her killed."

"So you had a motive for killing him."

Anna averted her eyes and her shoulders slumped forward. She did not answer the question. The courtroom was quiet. Then she looked up and shrugged. "Yes, I did."

"But you didn't murder the senator, did you?"

"No, I didn't."

"Tell us what was going through your mind as you held that gun on Senator Levall." The defense attorney smiled at her.

"He was angry when he came in that day, and I was scared. But... I-I just wasn't going to allow him to hurt me. Then... he, uh, he pulled the gun out. I looked in his eyes and knew he was going to kill me." Her voice grew stronger. "Just like he did my sister. The anger welled up inside of me, and I didn't feel afraid anymore. So when he came at me, I fought him. Everything happened so fast, and the next thing I knew I was looking down the barrel of that gun at him." She looked at the defense attorney. Tears moistened her eyes. "I watched the blood dribble from his nose and down to his lip. I couldn't take my eyes off of it. It lingered there, and I watched...and I knew I couldn't do it. I couldn't pull that trigger. But I wanted him to think I would. Wanted him to be afraid of me the way I was of him, the way Tina was when she died." She turned to the jury, imploring them with her eyes to understand what she tried to tell them. "If I was going to kill Ken, I would have done it as soon as I had my hands on that gun, but I didn't."

"Anna, you testified just now that if you were going to kill the senator, you would have done it as soon as you got your hands on the gun, and yet you cocked the gun. It seems to me if you weren't going to shoot him, you would not cock the gun. So why did you do it, Anna? Why did you cock that gun?" His voice became louder and stern, almost as if accusing her.

She didn't seem upset at this assault. She bowed her head, her hair falling forward to cover her face. A muttering filled the courtroom but soon dissipated with the glaring stare of the judge. When the courtroom had quieted, she looked up, turned to the jury and met their stares with an unwavering gaze. She sighed.

"It was that drop of blood, that damn drop of blood that rolled out of his nose and down his upper lip and just sat there on his lip. You probably can't understand how I felt, but it was as if I was in a trance. I couldn't take my eyes off of it." Her body jerked in a silent sob. "It just sat there, hanging from his lip, and he didn't even wipe it away. I kept waiting for it to drop, but then it rolled over his lip and into his mouth. He'd ignored it for so long I didn't expect it when he reached up to swipe at it. It scared me, and I cocked the gun in case he tried to grab me again. After that everything happened so fast. I felt my arm being bumped. Then Ken fell to his knees. It's so strange because I don't remember the gun going off. My arm jerked, and Ken was on his knees... on his knees." Her voice faded. She shook her head as if to clear it. "I dropped the gun as he slid to the floor. I couldn't believe it." She repeated herself in a softer undertone. "I just couldn't believe it."

The defense attorney gave her time to pull herself together. After a bit, he gently said, "Would you like to continue now, Anna? We can take a short break if you like."

"No," she said, "no, let's continue."

"Did you or Detective Mentz have a gun that night?"

"No. I don't own or possess a gun. I had my arms around John. If he'd had a gun on him, I would have known it. The only gun was the one Ken brought with him."

"Your relationship with Detective Mentz was not an intimate one, was it?"

"No."

"Are you in love with him?"

"I don't know … well … yes, I am."

"Anna, you said you cocked the gun, is that right?"

She nodded.

"I need a verbal response, please." Davis said.

"Yes, I did."

"Are you sure you didn't pull or put any pressure on the trigger?"

"I am definitely sure of that!"

"Did Detective Mentz pull or put any pressure on the trigger?"

"As God is my witness, neither one of us pulled that trigger." Her soft voice carried well across the quiet courtroom.

"Thank you, Anna, that is all." He turned to the prosecutor. "Your witness."

* * *

Hawthorne stood up, ruffled through some papers, and then walked to the witness stand. "Anna," he said, "what happened after the Senator fell to the floor?"

She looked at him with surprise on her face. "Why, we called the police, of course."

"I see. You didn't remove any evidence from the scene or change anything around, did you?"

"No."

"Tell me, when you discovered what the Senator was up to, why didn't you just leave him?"

Anna bowed her head and put her hand over her mouth. Lowering her hand, she looked at the prosecutor. "I was giving him my loyalty after all he had done for me. I just couldn't believe he could or would do such a thing. Not without proof that it was true. By the time I realized that what my sister was telling me was real, it was too late. Too late for my sister; too late for me to make it right."

"Were you angry?" Hawthorne said in a gentle tone.

"Of course I was but at myself." She sighed. "Yes, I was mad at Ken, but if I had listened to my sister to begin with, maybe things would have turned out differently."

"Did you and Detective Mentz concoct a story to tell the police that would vindicate you and put the blame on Detective Mentz?"

"Oh, no way. No, we didn't. I would never have allowed that, and John wouldn't have either."

Hawthorne turned and walked toward his table, stopping mid-stride. He paused before turning back to her.

"Anna, don't you have any regrets at all? Shouldn't you take some of the blame?" His voice held a tone of accusation, a tone that said she was guilty.

"You bet I do." Her face displayed her grief. "I didn't kill Ken, but in a way I killed my sister because I didn't believe her. I'll have to live with that guilt for the rest of my life. That won't be easy." She did nothing to wipe away the tears that flowed down her face, and eyes filled with pain stared back at him.

The prosecutor stood looking at her for a moment before saying, "I have no more questions for this witness, Your Honor."

Chapter 28

"Your Honor, the defense would now like to call Roger Hamrick to the stand."

The witness walked through the old wooden doors of the courtroom. Faces turned to view this man with curiosity.

The crow's feet at the corner of his faded blue eyes and the white mustache gave him a gentle, grandfatherly appearance. He strode to the stand confidently.

After being sworn in, the witness sat in the chair. The defense lawyer sauntered to the witness stand and placed one hand on the banister.

"Mr. Hamrick," he said, "please tell the jury what you do for a living."

"Yes, sir. I am the Director of the North Carolina State Forensics and Pathology Department, a division of the North Carolina State Law Enforcement. I have been with that department for the past thirty-five years."

"Thank you. Are you familiar with this weapon?" Attorney Davis handed him the plastic bag containing the gun.

After examining the gun, Mr. Hamrick replied, "Oh, yes. It's a Smith & Wesson .38 Special."

"That's correct. In your opinion, sir, do you think it is possible under certain circumstances that this gun could unexpectedly discharge?"

"Well, sir, it is not only my opinion, but it is also my experience that it could."

"Your experience?"

"Yes, sir."

"Would you please tell the court about this experience?"

"Last summer I went to the shooting range to practice. I had my 9mm Glock and a Smith & Wesson .38 Special. I decided to start with the .38. I had the gun cocked and was sighting my target when another gentleman came up behind me. He reached around me before I realized what he was doing. I caught a glimpse of him out of the corner of my eye and figured he was laying some papers on the bar in front of me. And he was, but when he withdrew his arm, he slightly bumped mine. I never even touched the trigger, but the gun went off. I couldn't believe my eyes when I looked at the target and saw I had a perfect bull's eye."

"Are you sure you never pulled that trigger or at least put a little pressure on it?"

"No, sir. I was still sighting my target. I wasn't ready to fire the gun."

"Thank you, Mr. Hamrick." The defense lawyer turned to the prosecutor. "Your witness."

The chair scraped against the floor as the prosecutor got up from his chair. He smiled at the witness. "Mr. Hamrick, did you, while sighting your target, have your finger on the trigger?"

"My finger was close to the trigger but was not touching it. I definitely was not applying any pressure to the trigger."

"I understand, but isn't it possible that when you were bumped you could have applied enough pressure to the trigger to fire the gun?"

"No, sir, no way."

"When you are sighting your target, do you concentrate completely on what you are doing?"

"I concentrate on it, sure, but not to the point that I would not realize I had pulled the trigger. I'm always well aware of what I'm doing when I have a gun in my hand."

"I see." The prosecutor turned to the judge. "I have no more questions of this witness, Your Honor."

The defense attorney got up quickly and said, "Your Honor, I have one more question of this witness."

"Go ahead."

"Mr. Hawkins, when this man bumped your arm, were you able to maintain your concentration, or did it distract you?"

"Oh, it definitely broke my concentration. That's why I pulled my finger away from the trigger."

"Thank you. That is all I have for this witness."

* * *

The defense attorney shuffled his papers around as the court waited patiently. When he found what he was looking for, he looked up and cleared his throat.

"I apologize, Your Honor, for the delay. Defense would now like to recall Dr. David Mercer to the stand." Davis watched the witness as he made his way to the witness stand, a thoughtful look on his face.

"Dr. Mercer, you had testified that, in your opinion, a Smith & Wesson .38 Special would *not* be apt to discharge upon being bumped, even with it cocked. Am I correct?" Davis reviewed his notes he held in his hand.

"That's correct."

"Your Honor, this was covered earlier in testimony. Is this really necessary?" The prosecutor rose quickly from his seat.

"Yes, Counselor, that's a good point." The judge turned to Attorney Davis with raised eyebrows.

"Defense held the right to recall this witness," Davis said. "If you will just give me a chance, Your Honor, I will tie this together for the court."

"Make sure you do, Counselor."

Davis glanced at the jurors as he said, "Thank you." He turned back to the witness.

"Dr. Mercer, you were present in this courtroom during the testimony of Detective John Mentz and Anna Kayce. Is this accurate?"

"Uh, yes." Mercer's eyes flickered to the prosecutor as if wanting him to help.

"And you were present during the testimony of Roger Hamrick and his account of his personal experience with a Smith & Wesson .38 Special, is this right?"

Once again Mercer glanced nervously in the direction of the prosecutor. He wriggled around in his chair without answering the question.

"Dr. Mercer," Attorney Davis said, "would you please answer the question. I don't believe the prosecutor can help you with it."

"Your Honor, I object." The prosecutor cried out angrily.

"Sustained," the judge said. "Counselor, stick to business, please."

"I apologize, Your Honor." With that the defense attorney turned back to the witness. "Dr. Mercer, you've been present in the courtroom and heard all the testimony given, correct?"

"I, uh...oh, hell, yes, I was present." Perspiration covered his forehead. He pulled out a plain handkerchief and wiped his face. Instead of putting it back in his pocket, he held it with both hands, first twisting it one way, then the other direction.

"Now then, I would like to ask you once again, do you think it is possible for a Smith & Wesson .38 Special to discharge if its own accord if the hand and/or arm of the hand that is holding the gun is accidentally bumped, especially if the gun has been cocked?"

Complete silence shrouded the courtroom as people waited for an answer. Even the judge leaned forward in anticipation.

"Well," Mercer said, "I still don't think it's probable, but I guess it is possible."

The courtroom broke out into a clatter of noise as the spectators turned to talk with one another about the significance of the answer, and the judge pounded his gavel until order returned. The prosecutor closed his eyes and bowed his head, while the defense attorney gave a big smile.

When the room was quiet, Davis said, "Defense is through with this witness, Your Honor."

"No, Your Honor, no questions." The prosecutor had a look of disgust on his face.

"Then the defense rests." Davis sat down and leaned back in his chair, a very self-satisfied grin on his face.

Anna realized she was holding her breath and exhaled slowly. Did she dare hope?

Best wait…wait and see where this goes.

She glanced at John. His face was expressionless. He looked thin and tired. It tore at her heart to see him like this.

He did this for me. I don't deserve it.

She picked up her purse and jacket, joining the crowd of people filing out of the courtroom.

I'm so tired of waiting. So tired…

Chapter 29

The next day court reconvened for closing arguments. Standing room only remained in the courtroom, and the atmosphere was subdued.

By arriving early, Anna managed to obtain a seat in the front. She wore a dress printed with tiny mauve roses and green leaves and an off-white sweater thrown around her shoulders. Her face was pale and drawn as she leaned forward and spoke with John for just a moment. As she did, a camera flashed. She turned and frowned at the reporter without speaking. Defense Attorney Davis leaned toward John and spoke into his ear. Without another word, John turned his back to her.

The bailiff called the court to order, and the Honorable Judge Talbot took his place. "Gentlemen, are you ready for your closing arguments?" The judge looked at both attorneys.

The prosecutor said, "Yes, Your Honor, I'm ready."

The defense attorney, still pulling papers out of his briefcase, said, "Yes, Your Honor, defense is ready."

"Then defense may proceed," Judge Talbot announced.

"Thank you, Your Honor." The attorney stood as he spoke and walked to the jury box, giving the jurors a sweeping glance.

"The scenario the prosecutor will present to you is correct except for a couple of things. First, this was not a premeditated act. Neither John Mentz nor Anna Kayce had any way of knowing that the senator would show up at Anna's apartment that night. There is no evidence presented to indicate they had in any way planned his arrival at her apartment. In fact, they had reason to believe the senator had possibly been or shortly would be arrested. There has to be premeditation for a verdict of first degree murder.

"Second, when Detective Mentz grabbed for Anna's hands, which held the gun, he did *not* do it with the intent to pull the trigger but with the intent of *preventing* the murder of the senator. Anna, defending herself, had cocked the gun. John touching her arm or hands was enough of a jar to cause the gun to discharge. It was an accident, and yet my client confessed to murder. Why? Why would he confess? He's a trained policeman, loyal to his duty to uphold the law. He was so sure it was his act of grabbing Anna's hands which caused the gun to discharge that he thought he was guilty. That is why he confessed. The truth is he was trying to prevent Anna from killing the senator. Her fear was driving her, and he knew she was not thinking straight—could not think straight. Everything happened so fast. He didn't have time to realize she probably would not pull that trigger.

"Think about it. If she really wanted to kill the senator to revenge her sister's murder, she would have pulled that trigger as soon as she picked up the gun or at least shortly thereafter." He paused, giving the jurors time to absorb what he said, then continued, emphasizing each word as he spoke. "But she didn't. She was holding the gun, pointing the gun, but there was a period of time between when she picked up the gun and when Detective Mentz grabbed for it. When it came right down to it, she could not pull that trigger." The defense attorney paced back and forth in front of the jury box, his eyes ablaze with emotion.

"When Detective Mentz was shot, he saw the senator's car, recognized it as the senator's car, and even saw the senator come out of the bushes and get in that car. But he did not want revenge for the shooting. Remember he is a professional, used to living dangerously, used to the possibility that he could be injured or even killed in the line of duty. No, the thought of revenge did not enter his mind. He wanted the senator to pay legally for his crimes.

"Where there is a reasonable doubt, you cannot by law bring a guilty charge." He paused again, allowing his statement to register. "I have presented you with a witness, who, through his own experience, held a gun in his hand, a gun just like the weapon owned and brought to the scene by the senator. A cocked gun that discharged of its own volition when Anna's arm was accidentally bumped. It's true there were the hands of two people on or near the weapon that night. It's true my client confessed that he may have been the one to cause the gun to discharge, killing the senator."

His voice grew stronger as he continued. "But it's not true that he pulled the trigger with deliberate intent to kill the senator. The gun was cocked and accidentally discharged when Detective Mentz grabbed for Anna's hands to pull the gun up and away from the senator. I have shown you, with a witness who experienced it himself, that this is possible."

He knew he had the attention of everyone in the courtroom, but the jury was his main focus. He maintained his visual survey of the jury, pacing back and forth in front of them. After a moment, he stopped.

"*There* is your reasonable doubt, clear and simple," he said, turning his back on the jurors, and walking with confident steps back to his table.

The bailiff handed the judge a note. Judge Talbot glanced at the clock after reading the note. "We will recess for lunch while I take an important phone call. Court will reconvene at one p.m. to hear the prosecution's closing argument."

* * *

Anna made her way to the hallway outside the courtroom. Unable to sit down and relax, she paced the floor and avoided the glances of the people walking by.

"Anna." The voice was so soft she almost didn't hear it. Turning around she found herself face to face with the prosecutor.

"Yes?" She flashed an uncertain smile.

"Are you really going to let him go to jail for this murder?"

"What?"

"Tell the truth, Anna. Don't let this man go down for this. He confessed, but you *know* who really did it."

"It was not murder. I'm telling you the truth. It was an accident." She glared at him, fists clenched tight.

"Tell the truth, Anna." Without a smile he turned and walked away.

* * *

The judge leaned forward and peered at the prosecutor over the top of his glasses. "Mr. Prosecutor, are you ready for your closing argument?"

"Yes, Your Honor, I am." The prosecutor ambled toward the jury and smiled, allowing his eyes to meet each juror's gaze.

"Detective John Mentz and Anna Kayce met during his investigation of a drug ring thought to be instigated and led by Senator Kenneth Levall. They very quickly became lovers, whether it was physical or emotional is unknown and, frankly, doesn't matter. The senator, being an intelligent man, discovered their relationship and became jealous. At the same time, Tina Kayce, Anna's sister, discovers the senator's little sideline in drugs and urges Anna to leave him. When the senator finds out Tina's discovery, he has Tina killed. That was a mistake. Anna becomes obsessed with her sister's death and, rightly, blames the senator. Their relationship deteriorates while her trust in Detective Mentz grows. Then the fateful night arrives. The senator goes to Anna's apartment to convince her he didn't have her sister murdered and hopefully win his mistress back. Detective Mentz hides in the bedroom while Anna has her confrontation with the senator.

"While the detective is in that bedroom, he comes up with a plan to get rid of the senator once and for all. He knew the senator always carried a gun. All he has to do is cause the confrontation to escalate to the point where he can get his hand on that gun and shoot the other man. But fortune smiles on him. Anna and Ken's argument does escalate. The senator pulls a gun. This gives John Mentz a good reason to pull his gun, but before he could, Anna wrestles with the senator and knocks the gun out of his hand. Reacting quickly, she retrieves the gun and points it at the senator. Detective Mentz, fearing the senator might escape, decides to end the whole situation, comes behind Anna, covers her hands with his, and presses against her trigger finger. Two fingers on that trigger."

The prosecutor pauses, his eyes sweeping the jury box, and allows the jury to absorb the information. "*Two* fingers on that trigger. The gun discharges, and the senator falls to the floor dead. That, my friends, is the real description of the crime, just as it happened. It was deliberate and intentional. It was... cold-blooded murder." The prosecutor looked at each juror while the silence in the courtroom grew, allowing the tension to increase, allowing the scenario he had presented to sink in. Then he turned his eyes from the jury and cast his gaze upon the spectators before continuing.

"And of course there's the little incident when Detective Mentz was shot outside Anna Kayce's apartment building. He truly believed Senator Levall was the one who shot him. Now I have no evidence one way or the other, so I can't say for sure who shot Detective Mentz, but the point is he believed it. Reason for him to also have a personal reason for wanting that gun to discharge and kill the senator, a reason for a personal vendetta.

"It has been my duty to prove beyond a doubt that Senator Kenneth Levall was murdered with cold intent. I have provided the weapon, proven by ballistics and even admitted to by the defendant and Anna Kayce to be the gun that killed the senator. It is the murder weapon without a doubt. I have given you two motives and even provided an expert witness with years of experience who testified, in his opinion, it was a slim probability that gun could go off accidentally. Now it is up to you, the jury, to bring justice to the senator by bringing in a verdict of guilty for first degree murder."

The prosecutor gave a confident nod of his head as if giving the twelve people in front of him his vote of confidence that they would do what he implored them to do. Then slowly he turned and walked back to his table.

The judge instructed the jury on the law for first-degree and second-degree murder and gave them instructions. "You are to go about your deliberations with an open mind, and do not form any final opinions too early. I must remind you not to talk to anyone about this case until you have reached your verdict. The clerk will now give you your verdict forms, and the bailiff will escort you to the jury room where you will elect a foreman before beginning deliberation."

After the jury left for the jury room, Anna waited in her seat while the courtroom emptied. John remained seated at the defense table while his lawyer spoke to him. When the aisle cleared, she slipped to where John sat. His lawyer shuffled through some papers while John held his head in his hand, elbow propped on the table.

"Hi," she whispered.

John looked up and smiled at her. "How're you doin'?"

"I'm okay. Are you holding up?"

"Yeah, I'm tough."

"I know, but it's still a lot to go through."

He shrugged. "Aw, it'll all be done with someday, and we'll look back and laugh about it."

"I don't think so." She frowned at him. "What does your lawyer think about how things are going?"

"Well, his only comment is we have a fifty-fifty chance of winning or losing."

"Oh." Anna sounded subdued.

"Anna?"

"Yes?"

He hesitated, gazing intensely into her eyes. "Oh, nothing."

"Thanks, John, for doing what you did for me."

"You're welcome." His grin was weakly boyish. "But I didn't do anything."

"Good luck, John."

He gave her a tired smile.

She turned and walked away, aware of his eyes following her.

* * *

While the jury began their deliberations and the waiting began, Anna decided to return to her apartment. Since the media crowded around the attorneys, Anna left unobtrusively and reached her car unnoticed.

She entered a quiet apartment. The sun shone in the window, warming the place too much. Anna opened the balcony doors to allow fresh air into the room. She remained in the doorway of the balcony, feeling the slight breeze sweep over her, caressing her body.

The doorbell rang. Anna opened the door and stared at the man in front of her. Striking blue eyes stared back at her. He was tall, and his broad shoulders filled the doorway. A rebellious blond curl fell over his forehead.

"Yes?" Anna said, feeling a sudden sadness.

"Hi," he said, his voice deep and hesitant. "I'm looking for Anna Kayce."

"You're speaking to her."

"My name is Daryl Carson. I knew Tina."

Tears filled Anna's eyes. Unable to speak, she stepped aside and waved him into her apartment.

He stepped inside and turned to her. "Something's happened to Tina, hasn't it?"

"Yes," she said. "Please, have a seat. We need to talk."

He perched on the edge of the sofa and turned to face her.

Anna followed suit, preferring to be more comfortable but knowing she would not be able to talk to him if she settled back into the cushions. "I'm sorry, but before I tell you about her, I need you to tell me how you came to know Tina." Her voice broke.

"Well, we haven't known each other very long, but we seemed to really click from the beginning. We met one night at a coffee house downtown. They were having a poet's reading, and I decided to read some of my work." He gave her a pleading look. "I love her, Anna. I want to spend the rest of my life making her happy if she'll let me. If that sounds corny, I'm sorry. It's just the way I feel."

Anna's chin trembled, but she managed a small smile. "No, Daryl, it doesn't sound corny at all. I think it's wonderful."

"Something's wrong with Tina, isn't it?"

"Yes, I'm afraid it is." She hesitated, not sure how to proceed. Anna forced herself to say the words. "Tina was murdered, Daryl."

"What?" He shook his head. "No, no, that can't be."

"I'm afraid so." She took his hand in hers. "It's a long story." When finished, she took a deep breath and slowly exhaled. "If only I had listened to her at first, maybe she would be alive today."

He remained quiet with his head down, the minutes ticking away. After a bit, he looked up at her. "Thanks for telling me. I should've been here for her, but business took me to Paris. I just got back yesterday. I've been trying to get in touch with her ever since." He appeared lost and not sure what to do.

"Do you mind if I ask you a question?" Anna said.

"Anything," he said, rubbing his eyes with his hand.

"Tina had mentioned you had given her a gift. What was it?"

"Oh, that. It was a music box I had gotten her while in Paris. It was handmade. I had it mailed to her so she would get it quicker. I wasn't sure when I would get back to the States." He looked at Anna with saddened eyes. "I guess it wasn't much, but she seemed to like it."

"I think she did, Daryl. She sounded excited about showing it to me."

"My life is really going to be empty now."

"It's going to take a while to get over it," she said, "for both of us."

"I'm not sure how to do that."

"Time, Daryl. Just give it time."

Dejected, he left, leaving Anna to her own grief. She walked out to the balcony and looked up at the sky.

Please, God, let this turn out all right for John.

Chapter 30

A few days later court reconvened. The jury filed into the courtroom and took their seats. The foreman of the jury took his place with the paper holding their verdict in his hands.

Prosecutor Hawthorne turned around and looked at Anna. Their eyes met and held. Anna looked away first, her hands picking nervously at a fold in her skirt.

The courtroom hushed. Anna turned her attention to John. His neck and jaw flexed with the stress he felt, while a wet line of perspiration saturated the edge of his shirt collar.

Judge Talbot leaned forward in his chair. "Has the jury reached a verdict?"

"We have, Your Honor," the foreman replied.

"Please give the court your verdict."

"We, the jury, in the matter of the State of North Carolina versus John Mentz on the count of murder in the first degree find the defendant not guilty. On the count of murder in the second degree, we find the defendant not guilty..." The cheers of the people in the courtroom obliterated the rest. Flashing lights from media cameras filled the room. Judge Talbot pounded his gavel, demanding quiet.

Anna took a deep breath and slowly released it. It was the first smile she had had on her face in a long time.

* * *

Anna didn't see the scowl on the prosecutor's face nor the dark look he turned her way. He turned back to his table, gathered his papers and shoved them into his briefcase. His mind had already gone on to his next case.

* * *

A flash went off in her face, bringing Anna back to the present. Without a word she turned her back on the media and made her way through the crowded hallway until she found an empty hallway. She slipped through the double doors and sighed in relief at escaping the crowd with their stares and whisperings. Leaning against a wall, she wondered what she would do with herself now. Life would not be the same, and Anna already felt the emptiness.

Curious, she eased the hallway door open enough to see and watched John raise his hands as if trying to ward off the reporters while the flash of cameras lit up around him. Putting himself between John and the cameras, his lawyer captured the media's attention, allowing John to avoid the crowd. Anna turned away from the door and the commotion, glad that John had escaped, also. She walked to a window overlooking a small courtyard to wait until the crowd cleared. The doors behind her swung open, and somehow she knew John was there.

"Anna."

She turned at the sound of his voice.

"Congratulations," she said.

"Yes, I was lucky."

"I'm glad."

"Anna?" He moved closer to her and clasped both her shoulders with his hands, pulling her to him.

She waited, saying nothing.

"I'm sorry, but I have to ask you. Did you pull that trigger?" His voice was barely above a whisper

"I can't believe you asked me that." She cocked her head to one side and looked at him, unsmiling. Her pain etched lines in her face. "What do you think?" she asked bitterly.

"I don't think you did, but..."

"But?"

"I love you, Anna." He held his hands up to her, palms up. "Please understand. I just need to hear you say it."

"I didn't do it, John. As God is my witness, I promise you I didn't pull that trigger."

He sighed and gave a boyish grin, slipped his arms around her, and buried his face in her neck.

She stood there for a moment, feeling emotions tugging at her heart. Then she encircled his neck with her arms.

"I love you, too," she whispered in his ear.

Acknowledgments

I would like to thank the following people for all their help, support, and suggestions. Very special thanks to Larry for the most valuable and extensive information he gave me pertaining to the undercover world of drugs and being an undercover agent. Special thanks to my good friend and fellow writer, Elysabeth Eldering, for all the help, support, and information she has provided during the writing of this novel. My gracious gratitude to Gene Lovely, a longtime friend and supporter, for his help in reading, pointing out typos and mistakes, and providing great suggestions. He has made a great editor. Thanks to Carol Franks, Brenda Whisenhunt, and all the other friends and family for their support. It has meant more to me than you will ever realize.

Finally my dream has been realized.

About the Author

Faye Tollison has loved mysteries for as long as she can remember. After 27 years in the medical field, she decided to devote herself to writing her own mystery.

She has written several articles on writing, which were published in The Quill and a short story published in Catfish Stew, an anthology by the South Carolina Writer's Workshop of which she has been a longstanding member. As a member in her local chapter of the SCWW, she wrote a number of critiques, and they were published in the chapter's newsletter, Printed Matters.

Faye resides with her three cats in upstate South Carolina and is presently writing her second mystery novel.

Made in the USA
Charleston, SC
04 October 2011